THE SHADOW
ON THE HOUSE

THE SHADOW ON THE HOUSE

Mark Hansom

RAMBLE HOUSE

The Shadow on the House by Mark Hansom
Introduction © 2009 by John Pelan

ISBN 13: 978-1-60543-346-2

ISBN 10: 1-60543-346-2

Cover Art: Gavin L. O'Keefe
Preparation: Fender Tucker

DANCING TUATARA PRESS #3

THE SHADOW ON THE HOUSE

Introduction by John Pelan

Welcome to one of the finest novels of psychological horror of the last century . . . That this novel is being reprinted should surprise no one. That a masterpiece of this calibre should have remained out-of-print and known only to the cognoscenti of the horror genre for seventy-five years is more than a little puzzling. Perhaps the most surprising element of all is that this book was the debut novel of a gentleman who went on to author several novels of equal merit and then after four years, seven novels, and one short story vanished as suddenly as he had appeared.

To present a convincing portrait of the darkest and most aberrant workings of the human mind is a difficult feat. In this arena Mark Hansom can stand as a peer with the likes of Peter Straub, Robert Bloch, and Ramsey Campbell. All of the above have offered up seminal works of psychological horror wherein the reader almost expects to find a supernatural agency at work. Writing a novel that relies on the perspective of a protagonist who may or may not be not be wholly reliable isn't an easy feat to pull off. Relevant details must still be conveyed to the reader and even if the protagonist is mad as a hatter, the standard conventions of the horror mystery novel still need to be adhered to. In other words, while his perspective of other people may be skewed by his insanity, descriptions of their actions as relevant to the story must be scrupulously described so as to not "cheat" the reader.

Bloch gave us *Psycho* after two decades of writing short stories of both supernatural and non-supernatural horror. Ramsey Campbell spent a long apprenticeship writing pastiches of H.P. Lovecraft's Cthulhu Mythos stories before offering up such masterpieces as *The Face that Must Die* and *The Doll Who Ate His Mother*. Peter Straub began his career as a gifted poet, progressed to novels and short stories and had a substantial body of work behind him by the time he launched the remarkable series of "Tim Underhill" stories that includes *Koko*, *The Throat* and several other pieces.

Mark Hansom submitted his credentials to join this august company with his very first work of fiction. *The Shadow on the*

House would be an impressive book under any circumstances. The characters are fully realized (even if everyone isn't exactly who or what they seem to be); the plot moves along briskly with no wasted scenes and as the oppressive sense of impending doom grows stronger the astute reader is able to piece together the clues that have been presented throughout the story and come to certain conclusions about the main characters just as the author pulls the curtain aside and reveals all.

The Shadow on the House has the distinction of being Hansom's only novel that was published in the US as well as the UK during his lifetime (in 2002, Midnight House published a new edition of *The Beasts of Brahm*, which is still available from the publisher. E-mail jpelan6@msn.com for details. Ramble House customers may purchase the book for the discount rate of $35.00 postpaid simply by saying "Fender sent me" in their e-mail). *The Shadow on the House* was also cited by the late Karl Edward Wagner as one of the thirty-nine best horror novels of all time. However, it is the opinion of this writer that at least two of his later novels were even superior. Mr. Wagner did confide to me that at the time his article and list appeared, he had read no other Hansom novels; so it's quite possible that had his article appeared a few years later Hansom may well have been represented with a couple of additional entries.

So who was this mysterious author whose star burned brightly for such a short time? The fact of the matter is that no one really knows for certain . . . Even though I was responsible for his entry in the encyclopaedia *Supernatural Literature of the World,* I was unable to include more than a brief bibliography and some conjectures as to what may have become of him . . . We do know that "Mark Hansom" was a pseudonym; there are no records of a person with that name being born (or dying) in the United Kingdom that could possibly have been the author. The man writing as Mark Hansom began his literary career in 1934 and his activity seemingly ended almost to the day that Great Britain entered the Second World War. Assuming that he was a young man in mid-to-late twenties at the time it's not at all unreasonable to think that he may have died in the service of his country. A colleague of mine proposed two theories as to his identity, the first is almost too absurd to comment on; namely, that "Mark Hansom" was yet another pseudonym of Charles Cannell (the author better known as "E. Charles Vivian" and "Jack Mann"). What makes this theory easy to refute is the great disparity in styles between the two authors.

Some of the indicators are the class-consciousness of Hansom; which implies a first-hand familiarity with the aristocracy and is a distinction completely ignored by Cannell. Secondly, anyone that has read Cannell under any of his by-lines will immediately see his fascination with aviation. One recurring motif in Cannell's work is that if airplane travel is involved, one is assured of a lengthy description of the plane, the mechanics thereof and possibly even the history of that particular model. If Hansom needs to use an airplane to move his characters from one place to another, we get no such descriptions; the airplane is merely a device to get the characters from point A to point B. Most definitely not the same person.

This same colleague also suggested that the obviously pseudonymous "Rex Dark" might also be Hansom. Other than the sheer illogic of using two different pen-names to sell the same sort of books (thrillers) for the same imprint, there's also the fact that "Rex Dark" was big on recurring characters and while Hansom used a recurring theme (killing off the villain early in the book only to have him return from the grave to wreak further havoc), he did not re-use his characters even though the opportunity presented itself. Lastly, and most importantly, I'll bring up that issue of class-consciousness once again. This is important as both a stylistic clue and very probably a clue to Hansom's identity. Mark Hansom writes of the upper classes and the unwritten rules governing the servants with the authority of someone writing from personal experience. There are indications that the man writing as "Mark Hansom" was of the upper rather than the lower classes.

One bit of circumstantial evidence is the fact that in the pre-WWII days, the publishing industry was still considered suitable employment for a gentleman, who while wealthy enough to not need to work was nevertheless encouraged to get a taste of the business world by working for a few years. An example would be Sir Charles Birkin, who served his apprenticeship in the business world as an editor for Philip Allan and as a result, brought out the justly famous "Creeps" series. The hint that Hansom may have worked in publishing is based on a rather odd set of circumstances . . . Some few years after their initial publication, Mellifont Press reissued all of his books, the last in 1951. What makes this a bit unusual is that Mellifont was a reprint house and while they did indeed publish a number of thrillers originally from Wright & Brown (including a few titles by "Rex Dark"), two of their selections by Mark Hansom were issued in abridged format. As it really isn't cost-effective to order up a re-write in such circumstances, one has to wonder if there was authorial involvement and if perhaps "Mark Hansom" was connected in some way to Mellifont Press? It could just as easily be that another employee of Wright & Brown made the move to Mellifont and recalled both Hansom and Dark as being among their more consistent sellers. The most unusual fact is the reprinting of *Master of Souls* in 1951, a full fourteen years after its initial publication. Generally speaking, Mellifont tried to get their reprints out within five years of a book's initial release in order to capitalize on any publicity the book had garnered (much as mass-market publishers do today). Publishing a paperback fourteen years after the hardcover just simply isn't done unless there's an editor really pushing the book.

So, this leaves us with two possible scenarios as to the fate of the man writing as "Mark Hansom". One of the many who died serving their country in WWII, or a life spent in the publishing business, perhaps affected so much by the horrors of war that he lost interest in the lesser horrors of the supernatural tale . . .

What we do know for certain is that he did leave a legacy of seven very fine novels a great novelette, and that at least five of these will see publication from Dancing Tuatara Press.

John Pelan
Midnight House
Summer Solstice 2009

THE SHADOW ON THE HOUSE

CHAPTER I

SYLVIA VERNON

I AM—OR WAS—the least superstitious of men; and when I managed to secure a place at Lady Somerton's dinner-table I thought I was doing merely a tremendously clever thing, in the manner of a young man who has not yet begun to take life seriously and who can find pleasure in bravado for bravado's sake.

There was nothing more in it than that. I thought what a grand thing it would be to be present at one of Lady Somerton's dinners—which were celebrated among those who set store by such vanities—and I managed to secure an invitation through the kindness of young Christopher Knight. I had no suspicion that the innocent matter of eating a dinner—even one of Lady Somerton's celebrated dinners—was to be more than a normal evening's entertainment; and I dressed with my usual care and set out in a taxi from my rooms in Brompton Road, arriving at Lady Somerton's Park Lane residence within a very few minutes,

It was a cold evening in October. The Park, immediately beyond the railings, was aglitter with the flashing lights of hurrying cars; but behind these lights—away under the trees—was mysterious darkness. It struck me then that we know very little of the world about us, for the darkness and mystery of the silent distance moved me to reflect upon the manner in which shadows affect us, and to wonder at the sinister atmosphere of trees brooding in the night.

But I soon dismissed these thoughts. Life to me then was an inconsequent affair of pleasure. I saw only lightness and gaiety, and deliberately hid my head in the sand to things of a morbid nature.

To that end I remember wondering how young Christopher managed to have the entree to Lady Somerton's, for the residence in Park Lane was not open to everybody, and Christopher, like me, was quite undistinguished in the world. And from that question, which was soon to be explained, I turned to speculation on the manner in which he had secured an invitation for me and, laughing to myself, wondered what sort of reputation I should be expected to maintain.

Christopher had not arrived when I was shown into the drawing-room. Lady Somerton was there, and, there were also present half a dozen elderly people who were probably distinguished but who, like all the distinguished people I have ever met, looked quite ordinary. And Sylvia was there.

I call her Sylvia now. But when I entered that drawing-room I had never set eyes upon her and had no anticipation of the profound emotional upheaval that was about to take place within me.

I saw a girl of the most unspeakable loveliness, and for the first moment of my setting eyes upon her I am afraid that I simply lost my normal self-restraint and stared at her, incredible. Perhaps I exaggerate. No one present seemed to be aware of my condition, and introductions were performed as though this divinely beautiful creature were any ordinary girl in any ordinary drawing-room, and as though I had not, in a moment, suffered a complete revolution of all my ideas of beauty, and as though life henceforth would not be a totally different thing for me.

I felt all these things, as I say. And I felt, also, that they showed in my manner.

But one thing I did not feel—the beginnings of tragedy. That seems a strange remark to make at this point in the narrative; but I have, since my first meeting with Sylvia, come to associate such beauty as hers with tragedy of the most terrifying kind.

I faced the introduction to Miss Vernon—Sylvia Vernon was her name—with what carelessness I could command. Fortunately she was one of the most unaffected girls I have ever met, and her friendly manner did all that could be done towards putting me at my ease. Had she cared to try to put me out of countenance by adopting a distant air I should have been quite thrown into confusion; but Miss Vernon was perfectly natural and I found myself conversing with her in a manner that surprised me after my utter bewilderment on first seeing her.

Lady Somerton, who had one of the most wonderful complexions I have ever seen, and whose expression always became delightfully animated when she spoke, left Miss Vernon and me together and hurried off to attend to some other of her guests.

"My aunt has been good enough to take me in hand," Miss Vernon told me when, with the precipitancy of youth, we had reached a personal footing in the way of conversation.

"Lady Somerton is your aunt?" I asked.

We had drawn aside, the two of us. We were the only young people present, and the other guests—three ladies and three gentlemen—were engaged with the hostess.

But though we had thus quickly arrived at a stage of pleasant familiarity, I was not the less affected by her amazing loveliness. She had been given a name and she had been given a voice and she had exchanged commonplaces with me and had even laughed at some happy remark of mine; but still she retained in the fullest measure that aura of impersonal beauty with which I had invested her. Her fair hair, her blue, sincere eyes, her slim dignity—these, in Miss Vernon, were mysteries that I could not understand. All that I could understand was that I had been translated into a higher sphere of emotional existence.

In short, I was hopelessly in love.

Lady Somerton now joined us. For this, strangely enough, I was grateful. No words of any importance had been exchanged between Sylvia Vernon and me (How could they, on such short acquaintance?), but I was afraid that my feelings must show through my banal conversation, and I was glad to be relieved by our hostess.

But of one thing I was certain: I should never rest happily until I had made Sylvia Vernon my wife.

A wild observation to make in the circumstances! A wild observation for even a very young man to make! But I made it, and I made it in all seriousness. That I had known her for less than ten minutes was a factor of no importance. That she was of a social status far above mine was likewise a factor of no importance. She had claimed absolute dominion over me. Nothing else mattered.

Then Christopher was announced.

At the mention of his name Sylvia looked up quickly towards the door and took an involuntary step forward, her eyes lighting up with a smile.

Lady Somerton went forward to welcome Christopher, and I was again left alone with Sylvia.

But now she was a different Sylvia. She was looking across the room, interestedly, expectantly, waiting for Lady Somerton to be finished with Christopher. Her lips were parted in a half smile. She was taking not the slightest notice of me.

I knew then how it was that Christopher—the undistinguished Christopher—had the entrance to Lady Somerton's mansion. And I knew what it was to be jealous.

Christopher came towards us, embracing both in his smile of greeting. But his eyes were devouring Sylvia almost all the time, and she accepted his admiration happily and returned it in full measure.

I joined in the conversation; but I had to force myself to act as though I enjoyed the position. And all the time I was telling myself not to be a boor, to congratulate Christopher—if only in my heart—for having succeeded so well as to win the love of such a singularly beautiful girl. But I could not force myself even to acknowledge that he had won Sylvia's love. She had taken me off my feet to such purpose that I could not contemplate her belonging to anyone else—even her belonging to dear honest Christopher who, as I should normally have admitted, was worthy of the finest girl in London.

"Mr. Strange has been telling me," said Sylvia, "that you and he are called 'the inseparables' at your club. It isn't at all nice of your friends to give you nicknames. I don't like nicknames. When they mean anything at all they are usually over-candid and seldom flattering. But what I want to remark is that if you are such good friends why is it that I haven't met Mr. Strange before this evening?"

"Easily explained!" said Christopher, running his hand over his fair curly hair. "There used to be a music-hall song (Of course, *you* haven't heard it!) which advised one never to introduce one's sweetheart to a pal. You should really ask why you are being allowed to meet Martin even now. I'm afraid I'm being guilty of folly in running against music-hall wisdom. For wisdom is to be found in the most unlikely places, you know."

It was then that we were summoned to dinner, and Christopher's remarks were immediately forgotten, I suppose, by both him and Sylvia. But they remained in my mind, for I could take them seriously.

Ten of us sat down to dinner. I was placed between a lady in black, who had a son in India, and a lady in pale blue, who had no son at all but who had five daughters; and the first three courses were spent in listening to these two—one of whom would have given the world to have her son back on her hands, while the other, so far as I could gather, would have given the world to have her daughters off hers.

Then someone—a Professor Wetherhouse, with whom I was to become more closely acquainted in the future—began on the subject of ghosts.

I was not interested in ghosts, any more than I was interested in rare sons or superfluous daughters.

But Sylvia, curiously enough, was interested in ghosts. She allowed her attention to wander from Christopher; and Christopher made a wry face at me across the table and assumed a comical expression of the most intense interest in the Professor's remarks.

The Professor said nothing original. He told us that he had never met anybody who had seen a ghost outside the darkened rooms of a spiritualist, and that he had never met any honest person who was not inclined to keep an open mind on the subject.

"But surely, sir, you don't believe in such things!" I ventured to remark.

I was slightly disturbed by the knowledge that such a hard-headed man as Professor Wetherhouse was reputed to be should pay any attention to old wives' tales.

"No, I don't believe," he said. "I didn't say I believed." He had a face that spoke of tolerance, and the tone in which he spoke took all the sharpness out of the rebuke which I had merited. "But I don't lay that I disbelieve," he added. "The most I can do is to reserve any opinion."

"Then you think that there might be some truth in the stories we hear about haunted houses and haunted families and all that sort of thing?"

It was Sylvia who spoke; and I noticed the curious way in which her voice trailed off towards the end of her sentence, and the way in which her lips were parted, and the way in which she kept her eyes on the old gentleman's face.

Christopher, too, was looking up—genuinely interested now. In fact, the three of us—the three youngsters—were more absorbed in the question than any of the others. We three were on the threshold of life. We found life a good thing, and it would be disturbing to be told that there were queer things going on about us—things that we did not understand, things that threatened the fine inconsequence of youth.

"There certainly might be," said the Professor; and there the matter disappointingly ended through someone butting in with a remark upon theatres.

But during the rest of the dinner Sylvia was quiet.

So was Christopher, probably because he could not engage Sylvia in conversation. And so was I. The temporary interest of the Professor's remarks had expended itself and I was once more thinking of the tremendous fact of Sylvia.

I could not see tragedy ahead, but I could see distressing complications. Christopher was my best friend, and he had won the affections of Miss Vernon. He was, of all men, the one most entitled to the affections of such a divine creature, but that did not count with me then. The only thing that did count was that I and not he should win her. I would have sacrificed everything— friendship, honour, my immortal soul—to that end. The mere sight of a girl had altered my very character.

Christopher and I left together. The night was cold but fine, and we set off to walk down Park Lane. At Hyde Park Corner we should part, he to go on to his rooms in Jermyn Street and I to stroll along to the Brompton Road.

"I ought to congratulate you," I said, "on having found such an exquisite creature as Miss Vernon."

"Ought to?"

"Yes. Unfortunately I can't. I've fallen in love with her myself."

He laughed.

"That's better than any congratulation," he said. "It's the most sincere compliment you could pay me. I am a lucky devil, eh?"

Christopher was so innocently proud of himself that I was almost ashamed of my jealousy.

It never occurred to me to observe that I was being despicably churlish in withholding my congratulations. I ought to have been happy for Christopher's sake, but I could not bring myself to share in his joy.

"You *are* a lucky devil," I agreed. "Do you know what I could do?"

"What you could do?"

"Yes . . . I could kill you."

It was not until the words were out of my mouth that I realized what I had said. Even then I might have laughed and turned such a terrible assertion into a jest; but I was struck aghast for the moment by the knowledge that I actually meant what I said.

Christopher might have laughed too, for it was inconceivable that he should take me seriously; but there must have been something in my expression or in my tone that made him guess at my true feelings, for he said:

"You don't mean that, of course?"

Again it was the tone in which the words were spoken that gave them their fullest meaning. The tone expressed uncertainty. He could not be sure that I did not mean what I had said.

Even then it would have been easy for me to laugh at his doubt and at the start of panic that had leapt to his eyes for just an instant. It would have been easy for me to laugh and so clear the air immediately.

But instead of that I tried to assure him by serious words that of course I did not mean what I had said.

"It was just a passing thought," I told him. "A temporary assertion of instinct over breeding, if you like. You know that the most peaceful of us sometimes want to kill."

"I understand. But why *should* you want to kill me?" he asked, laughing now, but glancing curiously towards me nevertheless.

"Because I am jealous of you, Christopher," I replied. "I am more jealous of you than I have ever been of anyone."

"Do you mean because of Sylvia?"

It was of no use my trying to deceive Christopher. To deceive him I should have had to deceive myself, and I knew I could not do that. Sylvia Vernon had made too great an impression upon me. Had I been less affected by the girl's unspeakable loveliness I might have kept my feelings hidden in my breast and might have suffered Christopher to go ahead with his wooing under my very eyes. But as things were, such self-restraint would have driven me mad.

I had to be frank with Christopher.

"Yes," I said; "on account of Miss Vernon. You and I know each other well enough not to worry about convention. I'm jealous of you, and I say so. I would sell my soul to be in your position. You know what that means!"

"I'm afraid I don't. What does it mean?"

I did not answer immediately. We walked on in silence for about fifty yards, then came to a standstill on the pavement of Piccadilly.

"It means," I said, laughing and laying my hand on his shoulder, "it means that I want a holiday. And the sooner I pack off, the better. I'm getting stale, nervy. Not enough variety. Want a change."

I had suddenly regretted my outspokenness. It would have been better, I now thought, had I not mentioned my feelings and had I simply made up my mind to go away. But I had had no intention of going away. I had intended to stay and fight my way into Miss Vernon's affections. I never doubted but what I could do so. Christopher's position had not troubled me so far as my being successful with Miss Vernon was concerned.

But my better nature asserted itself even while I was telling Christopher that I was jealous of him, and at the last moment I drew out—said I wanted a change. There was something about Christopher—his fine trusting honesty, perhaps—that prevented me from trying to rob him of Sylvia.

We bade each other good night there on the pavement of Piccadilly, having laughed away the shadow that for a moment had risen between us, and I turned and set off towards the Brompton Road.

And no sooner had I left him—freed myself from the influence of his presence—than I told myself that I was all manner of fools. My thoughts immediately began to play about the image of Sylvia Vernon. I saw her again in all the freshness of her maddening beauty. I heard again her soft musical voice, and was thrilled again by the enlivening effect of her personality.

Why should I trouble about scruples of honour?

Was it wrong to sacrifice even a friend like Christopher if it should mean my eternal happiness?

I asked my conscience these questions, and my conscience answered. But did I heed the answers? I did not. To me at that moment there was only one standard of right and wrong. Winning Sylvia was right, losing her was wrong.

I am not ashamed to say that. I suppose I ought to be; but so irresistible was the attraction that that slim girl exercised over me that I almost think myself freed from responsibility in the matter.

I went home to sleep and to dream.

CHAPTER II

AT JERMYN STREET

UNDER THE INFLUENCE of Sylvia I had expected to dream. That was quite a sentimental and poetical notion, of course, of the sort that comes to most young men, I suppose, when they are suddenly brought face to face with the most wonderful fact in the universe.

But I did not dream. On the contrary I slept as solidly as a log—too solidly, I think, for I awoke with a splitting headache.

I touched the bell at my bedside, and in a few seconds Makepeace—the man whose mission it is to overcome all the minor worries of my existence—entered the room with my morning cup of tea and two biscuits on a tray.

Makepeace has spent his life in the service of our family, and he clings to me even in this time of comparative poverty when the estates have gone to another branch of the tree and I am the sole survivor of the old stock beloved by Makepeace.

"I hope you slept well, sir."

"Too well, Makepeace," I replied. "I was never so ready for a cup of tea as I am now."

I thought that Makepeace looked at me curiously then, but it is difficult to pierce Makepeace's expression.

"I thought I heard you about in the night," he said, half apologetically. Then he added: "It must have been those dreadful people upstairs again. The pity of it!"

This last exclamation was made in reference to my having to occupy a very ordinary flat in a very ordinary building that rose directly from the pavement of a main street and that had a row of shops along the ground floor. This come-down in the world affected Makepeace much more closely than it affected me. It was his chief sorrow in life, and I could not argue it away. I might point out that unless I counted my pennies in the matter of rent I should not be able to retain his services, and I might try to prove that the Brompton Road was a very good road on the whole and that a bachelor such as I was not expected in these days to occupy a mansion in one of the Mayfair squares. But these arguments did nothing to alleviate his sorrow, and his answer to all my attempts at comforting him was: "But the shops, sir! To think that any member of the family of Strange should live over a shop!"

When he had left the tea and the biscuits by my bed and had returned to his duties I began to reflect upon the affairs of the night before, and especially upon my remarkable attitude towards Christopher.

Now, in the bright light of an autumn morning, I was amazed to think that my feelings had carried me so far as to make me object openly to Christopher's good fortune in being accepted as Sylvia Vernon's lover. My conduct seemed inexcusable now. I was still as much in love with Sylvia as ever, but my attitude towards Christopher had changed. I could curb my jealousy. I felt that it would be a grand thing to go along to his rooms and apologize for my boorish behaviour of last night.

Dear old Christopher deserved the best. I must not do less than congratulate him upon his immense happiness.

After breakfast I set out for Jermyn Street. I was extraordinarily happy. It might have been the thought of apologizing to Christopher that made me happy—that and the satisfaction of having overcome my churlishness.

I walked slowly, enjoying the crisp morning air and trying to dismiss the thoughts of Sylvia Vernon that would insist on coming forward into my mind. But I could not help being violently in love with her (I doubt whether any man could) and I could excuse myself for giving way to hopeless dreams. I took a morbid pleasure in these dreams—the morbid pleasure of the martyr.

It was about eleven o'clock when I reached Jermyn Street. The main door leading to the stairway common to all the chambers in the building stood open. It always was open. The place was let out in furnished suites of rooms to a number of bachelors of Christopher's stamp who came and went at all hours of the night.

As I turned into the doorway and started to ascend the staircase I felt in my pocket for the latchkey of Christopher's rooms. I had a latchkey of his rooms as he had one of mine. We had at times found that arrangement to be of great convenience.

Christopher's rooms were on the second floor. I had ascended to the first-floor landing when I heard voices above me; and, looking up, I could see that one or two people were on the stairway near Christopher's door.

I could see a silk hat held in someone's hand, and beyond that there was the suggestion of a brown fur coat.

I kept on up the ancient stairway, and when I came to the half-landing I could see that the owner of the silk hat was Professor Wetherhouse and that he had his free hand on the shoulder of the woman who wore the fur coat. She had her back towards me so that I could not see her face; but her head was bowed and the Professor seemed to be pleading with her.

So much I noticed at a first glance; and I also noticed that the door of Christopher's chambers stood open and that there was some sort of movement going on within.

At that moment the Professor raised his head and saw me. He recognized me at once; but it struck me as odd that there should be no smile of greeting in his glance. He seemed worried, and accepted my arrival as a thing of no moment in the midst of whatever it might be that was afoot.

Then the woman turned and looked at me.

It was Sylvia Vernon. She was crying, or had been crying. Her face was deathly white, and her eyes stared at me as though she were in the midst of some awful horror, as indeed she was.

"Here is Mr. Strange," said the Professor then, and patted her shoulder once more, giving the impression that my arrival might be some consolation to the girl. "Will you allow Mr. Strange to take you home? You ought not to have come, my dear. I told you how it would be."

"Is anything the matter?" I asked. It was a foolish question, but that was not the time to weigh words.

"Why, surely you've heard?" exclaimed the Professor. "They told me they had telephoned to you."

"I left home nearly an hour ago," I told him. "But what is the matter?"

He glanced furtively at Sylvia as though afraid to speak in front of her, then, taking her arm and beckoning me to follow, he led us through into Christopher's sitting-room.

There he put Sylvia into a chair, and me he guided over towards the window which overlooked Jermyn Street.

By this time I was in a state of the most painful expectation. As we had come through the little hall by which the several rooms of the suite communicated, the door of Christopher's bedroom had opened and two men had stepped forth. They had the professional air of doctors; and this with the unaccountable expression on Sylvia's face and the disturbed manner of Professor Wetherhouse had told me that something startling had taken place.

"Christopher is dead," said the Professor suddenly—so suddenly that I started back from the hand that he had raised to lay on my shoulder.

"Dead!" I exclaimed. "But he can't be dead."

I shall never forget the fine tact and humanity of the old man. He saw how the sudden news had shocked me, and instead of allowing it to have its full effect he drew me closer to the window and said:

"I want you to do what you can for Sylvia. It's bad enough for us—for you and me—but it's a thousand times worse for her. It's very distressing, but we must forget that. I was all against her coming here this morning when I heard the news (I happened to be along at Lady Somerton's), but she wouldn't be persuaded. See what you can do with her. Get her home. She can do nothing here."

These words steadied me. They got me over the first shock of hearing such terrible news.

Yet I was aghast. I could not speak. Christopher, who had parted from me last night on the pavement of Piccadilly in the full enjoyment of perfect health, to be dead! I could not grasp that. For a moment I stood staring out of the window, my perceptions shocked into dullness. Then, in a flash, I realized what I had been told. Christopher had simply ceased to be. His place was empty. His personality was but a memory. The living Christopher was no more.

I need not try to describe the sense of desolation that came over me at that moment, nor the sense of superstitious horror. I was young, I loved Christopher, and it was my first acquaintance with death.

"You mustn't let it affect you too much," the old professor was saying. "You must think of Sylvia . . . And I haven't told you the worst yet."

"The worst?"

"Yes. The circumstances are unusual. In fact—in fact—"

The Professor could not proceed. He stood for a moment biting his lip in agitation, then he suddenly turned.

"Come with me," he said quickly, and walked across the room.

Sylvia jumped up at his approach, and put out her hands as though to clutch the lapels of his coat; but he took her by the arms and gently forced her back into her chair.

"No, my girl," he said. "Please be guided by me! I ask you not to insist on seeing him. It would do no good. It would only upset you further. Wait here just one minute."

Sylvia allowed herself to be persuaded. She did not say one word in protest. It struck me then that she had not said one word since my arrival.

The Professor signed to me to follow him.

I did so with a queer nervousness working inside me. I would rather not have gone.

Immediately inside the door of the room there was a policeman. The sight of him shocked me indescribably.

And, sitting in a chair, staring into space, was Jepson, Christopher's young manservant.

A white sheet completely covered the bed, showing an outline horribly significant.

The place was unutterably still. The policeman did not move at our entrance. Jepson, staring into space, his chin cupped in his hands, his elbows on his knees, did not move. And the figure under the sheet lay with a stillness that was majestic.

Then, after a time, I found myself standing close beside the bed. The Professor signed to me to turn back the sheet. At first I could not. I could only stare.

I have already said that I regarded life lightly, and that I deliberately avoided morbid speculations. To me the idea of death had always been painful, and my subconscious mind had made me rather to scoff at all the mystery and awe with which death was surrounded. I argued that the mystery and the awe were due merely to ignorant superstition, that a dead man was essentially the same as a dead dog or a dead rat; and in my vast youthful vanity I was, of course, beyond being affected by ignorant superstition.

Alas for my materialism!

But I did at length muster up enough courage to draw back the sheet so that I might see the face of my friend.

I think I must have given an exclamation of horror, for, on turning away quickly, I saw that even Jepson had ceased from his staring and had risen and was coming towards me with a look of alarm on his face. Then I hid my face in my hands.

I understood the Professor's diffidence about telling me what had happened. And I realized that on no account must Sylvia Vernon be allowed to see what I had seen. Christopher had been murdered. He had been strangled. I shall not try to analyse the emotions that I suffered then. Let me say only that I experienced a revolting nausea and that I was filled with an unnameable horror.

It was bad enough to know that my friend was dead. But the ordinary sense of loss was entirely swamped by the terrible circumstances of his death.

He had died apparently after a terrific struggle, and his now fixed expression showed that his last moments had been filled with sheer terror. I refrain from giving the sickening details of his appearance.

After a time we returned to Sylvia, whom we found sitting exactly as we had left her. I had the curious sense of existing in a dream. I was not conscious of having to exert myself in order to move or to talk. Everything seemed unreal.

The Professor was pleading with Sylvia again, and I was adding a word now and again to his pleading; and at length Sylvia rose and took my arm and the three of us went down the ancient staircase.

In Piccadilly the Professor left us.

"Let's walk home," Sylvia had said. "I must be active."

These were the first words I had heard her speak that morning, and she said them with a sudden energy that seemed to show that she was determined to take a firm grip upon herself.

The Professor looked sharply at me, as though to see whether I were capable of being left in charge of a girl who had suffered as this girl had suffered, and then, evidently satisfied, he took his departure eastwards to fill an engagement that he mentioned.

"Are you sure you would rather walk?" I asked. "It's a good way. I'll call a taxi if you like."

"Do nothing of the sort," she said with a touch of impatience. "It's only a step. And I told you I wanted to be active."

So I fell in beside her, and we strode along in silence for some minutes.

"Why wouldn't Professor Wetherhouse let me see him?" she suddenly demanded.

It was not an ordinary question: it was a demand, and it suggested that she objected to being treated as a child in a matter of that sort.

"The Professor knows best," I parried. "I almost wish he hadn't allowed me to see him. You know the circumstances, of course?"

"He was murdered. I think the Professor would have kept that from me too, only they told us that on the telephone when they rang up this morning."

I was surprised by the control that she now had over her feelings. Of the two of us she seemed to have the firmer grasp over herself.

She had now let go of my arm, and was walking along independently by my side.

"His valet found him dead this morning when he went in to call him," she went on. "He had been strangled, I understand. Can you account for it at all?"

She spoke in an amazingly level voice, considering the dejected state in which she had been less than half an hour earlier.

Strange as it might seem I had not yet thought about that point. The death and the horrifying circumstances of the death had been in themselves the one overwhelming phenomenon. I had not related the death to anything beyond itself.

"No," I said. "I can't imagine who could have done it. He hadn't an enemy in the world so far as I know. Was it robbery, do you think?"

I was suddenly immensely curious about the reason for the murder. I regretted my not having been sufficiently master of myself to ask the Professor for practical particulars, for Sylvia's question made me realize that there was this other side to the matter.

"No, not robbery," she said. "The Professor told me that much just before you arrived. Jepson says that nothing has been disturbed. Shall we sit in the Park for a few minutes?"

We had crossed the road in the meantime, and instead of turning up towards Park Lane she raised her hand towards Hyde Park Corner.

I nodded, and we continued forward and entered the Park by the big gates.

The sun had taken the earlier crispness out of the air and it was now warm enough to sit. Beyond the shrubbery we found chairs in a not too exposed place under some trees.

"But don't you think Lady Somerton will be wondering what has become of you?" I asked. "In any case, won't it be better for you to go home?"

"Now, please!" she exclaimed. "Don't you try to treat me like a child as well. It was very kind of Professor Wetherhouse, I suppose, so far as his intentions went; but it is not very flattering—of either of you. I think I am as well able to withstand the shock as—as you are. I can forgive the Professor. He is old enough to have forgotten that young people have a peculiar capacity for withstanding such shocks."

I was thereby led to understand that Sylvia Vernon had a strength of character that her delicate appearance did not suggest; and I in turn gathered strength from her courage.

We spoke of other things. She told me about herself—how that Lady Somerton was her nearest relative, and how she had only recently come to London from Cambridge, and a number of other everyday particulars in no way connected with the tragedy of that morning. And as she continued to speak, the shadow of the tragedy became less oppressive, and it was difficult to believe that this was the girl who, such a short time ago, had been overcome with horror.

To me then it seemed almost callous of her to be sitting there chatting about inconsequent things. When I had gathered myself together at the Professor's request in order that I might be of assistance to Sylvia Vernon I had expected that my utmost tact would be required in the handling of a girl rendered frantic with grief. But her composure was perfect.

"You must come in to lunch," she said. "My aunt will be glad to see you, I am sure. This has been a terrible upset for her. It is really selfish of me to stay out for so long."

I said I should be delighted to be of any service.

But I was amazed at the marvellous way in which she had recovered her grasp on life. It struck me then that perhaps she had not been so completely in love with Christopher as I had been led to understand.

"You see," she went on, rising as she spoke, "my aunt is getting on in life. Such things are bound to affect her. She hasn't the ability to—"

She stopped suddenly.

We had both risen. Without warning she sat down again, and burst into the most violent fit of tears.

I sat down beside her, hurriedly, startled by this complete change in her manner.

"What is there to live for now?" she muttered distractedly, speaking, it seemed, to herself. I could not help overhearing, though her face was buried in the fur coat about her knees. "And he never harmed a soul! He never harmed anybody. He was the finest man in the world. Why should this happen to him?"

I tried to soothe her, but I could not. She, who but a moment ago had been deceiving herself with solicitude over Lady Somerton, was now completely heartbroken.

Somehow I was glad. I should have been intensely disappointed if this lovely creature had not had the weakness that she was now exhibiting.

In the midst of this paroxysm of weeping she straightened herself and turned to me, unashamed of the tears that were flowing down her cheeks.

"Don't leave me!" she pleaded. "The horror of it will drive me mad. He was your best friend, and he was mine. You and I know how splendid he was."

I promised. I promised readily. That seemed to go some way towards pacifying her. In a few minutes she said she would now return home.

And, feeling the clutch of her arm linked in mine, my thoughts flashed unbidden back to last night.

"What's the matter?" she exclaimed in alarm, stopping in her stride because I had stopped.

"Nothing!" I said earnestly. "Nothing!"

I could not tell her that last night I had for a mad moment been moved by elementary impulses so that I had wished his death.

I have already laboured the point that I was not superstitious; but from the instant of stopping in my stride a terrible superstitious fear took hold of me.

My prayer—for it had the force of a prayer—had been answered; and Christopher, the man who had possessed what I coveted with my whole soul, lay dead.

This was more horrifying than anything else.

CHAPTER III

PERSONS UNKNOWN

TWO OR THREE DAYS later I found myself in a long low room that was uncomfortably close and hot and that was lit by electricity, although the time was the early afternoon.

Sylvia was with me, and Professor Wetherhouse as well; and the three of us stood in the gangway by the wall because such seats as were there were crowded by what, in a court, is known as the public, as distinct from the officials and principals in the several cases to come under review.

"What are all these people here for?" asked Sylvia, holding my arm tightly and peering into the semi-darkness. "Surely they have nothing to do with the inquest?"

"Ours is not the only one," I told her. "But the most of these people are here to—out of curiosity."

"How horrible!" she exclaimed. "I wish I hadn't come."

"Do you want to go? There's really no need for you to be here."

"I should feel as though I were deserting him."

"No, no. The Professor will stay."

But the surprising creature, giving a shrug of abhorrence, decided to go through with the ordeal.

Fortunately ours was the first case to be inquired into.

The coroner was a fussy little man who seemed to be out of temper about something; and instead of coming to the matter in the reverential attitude that would have been in keeping with our feelings, he began by rating one of the minor officials because of some document that could not be found immediately.

It never occurred to us, I suppose, that perhaps the supreme matter of interest to the coroner was the failure of his son to pass an important examination, or the fact that his wife was insisting upon going to Switzerland or to Italy at a time when he could not afford to take her to Switzerland or to Italy. The tragedy of Christopher's death was to him not a tragedy but so much legal work to be got through before he could push on to some more legal work.

The only important witness called was Herbert Thomas Jepson, who gave evidence regarding the finding of the body of his master when he went to call him at half-past eight in the morning. Then Jepson told how he telephoned to the police and then to one or two of his master's intimate friends.

The coroner then asked Jepson one or two questions.

"At what time did your master come home on the previous night?"

"At about eleven o'clock, sir."

"Alone?"

"Pardon, sir?"

"I said, was he alone?"

"Yes, sir. He had been dining at Lady Somerton's, in Park Lane."

"And he retired immediately?"

"Yes, sir."

"Did he seem in his usual spirits?"

"I didn't notice anything unusual."

"Then he *was* in his usual spirits?"

"Yes, sir."

"Well, why don't you say so! You sleep in the flat, I understand?"

"I do."

"Did you hear anything in the night?"

"No, nothing."

"Now, correct me if I'm wrong. I understand that your master slept with his window open, and that the window, which is at the back, gives access to a flat roof, which in turn communicates by fire-escape ladders with the rest of the block of buildings in which your rooms are situated. It would be quite easy for anyone who wished to enter the room to enter it without having to use any force or any special skill."

Jepson nodded, and was then told to stand down but not to leave the court.

There then followed some sort of conclave amongst the officials and a shifting and coughing among the public, and this shifting and coughing was accompanied by a rising volume of chatter.

"Do you know," I whispered to Sylvia, "that he left almost the whole of his money to Jepson?"

"Yes," she said. "Do you think—"

An angry call for silence cut her words short.

"Is Lady Somerton present in court?" asked the coroner, with a glance at the clock on the wall.

Some of the public looked about them expectantly. Sylvia started, and clutched my arm nervously. There was a dead silence for some seconds.

Then I, on a sudden impulse, detached Sylvia's hands from my arm and walked towards the front of the court. The coroner looked up inquiringly at my approach.

I spoke to the first official I reached, telling him who I was and how I believed that I was the last of Christopher Knight's friends, except Jepson, to see him alive. My words were conveyed to the coroner, and after some deliberation and frowning and another glance at the clock he asked me to take the oath.

My evidence did not amount to much, but I was anxious that I might help in any way possible in the business of running the murderer to earth.

I told them that I had left Christopher at Hyde Park Corner at a quarter to eleven and that I had no reason to believe that he had an enemy in the world. I said that he had been in the highest of spirits all the evening. I also mentioned—for what reason I do not know unless it was a desire to put every relevant piece of news in the possession of the officials—that I had a duplicate key to Christopher's flat.

They dismissed me then, and I rejoined Sylvia and the Professor.

There was more talking, most of which I did not understand because my mind was occupied in sifting out the evidence on my own account and I could see that the authorities might jump to any one of three conclusions—namely, that someone had found the way in by the open window with the intention of robbery, had been disturbed by Christopher, had killed him in fear, and, panic-stricken, had made off empty-handed; or that Jepson had committed the crime, which to me was unthinkable; or that I, having easy access to the rooms at any hour of the day or night, had committed the crime.

I was forced to think of this last possibility, for the coroner had given me the impression of soulless officialdom. And, thinking of that, I was amazed to realize that were it to be suggested that I had visited Christopher's rooms in the middle of that fatal night I should be totally unable to prove the contrary.

The verdict of the jury was made known shortly afterwards. It was the expected one of murder by some person or persons unknown.

The relief of getting out to the street again from the closeness and semi-darkness of that sordid room with its reeking humanity was unspeakable.

The Professor left us and departed in a taxi, and once again I was given the duty of escorting Sylvia Vernon home.

She clung to my arm. There seemed to be nothing out of the ordinary in her doing so. She had known me for less than a week, but we had been thrown together in such intensely emotional circumstances that we had, without question, bridged all conventional gulfs and were more intimately familiar than we might have been after years of normal acquaintanceship.

It struck me then—for up to now my thoughts had been almost wholly concerned with the tragedy—that not only was Christopher dead (it seemed, as I had already realized, in answer to my accursed wish) but I was now in Sylvia's good graces, also in accordance with my wish.

Such materialism as I might still have possessed was not proof against that. I saw in these events the fearful hand of an inscrutable power. It seemed that I had only to wish and the wish was granted, and human life was not allowed to stand in the way.

The thought seemed fantastic, of course; but when one begins to speculate upon the supernatural there is no such thing as fantasy. With me there was only a strange terror because of the thought that there might be within me such an awful power as that suggested by the events.

As we turned to walk back to Park Lane—for Sylvia seemed to set much store by walking—I thought to tell her what was in my mind. Fear prompted me to drop her friendship. I had the feeling that either she or I was accursed.

But I delayed. Even the tragedy of Christopher and the effects of my private fear had not, even temporarily, blinded me to her extraordinary physical attractiveness; and though I could not dream then of taking advantage of the circumstances that threw her so much into my company, I could not, at the same time, refrain from being in love with her.

So I did not say one word of any of the thoughts that were in my mind.

CHAPTER IV

Cousin Mick

SIX MONTHS PASSED—six months that were uneventful except for the gradual strengthening of the ties that joined Sylvia and me—and I almost ceased to feel the effects of my recent experiences. I had not forgotten them, nor could I overcome the sense of tragedy when I thought of Christopher's early death. But I did not now *feel* the horror of that time. Most important of all, I had managed, I think, to dismiss the superstitious fears that had been born of the coincidence of my jealous outburst on the eve of the tragedy.

Time had enabled me to dismiss these fears, and I was lulled into peace. As though the supernatural takes account of time!

It now seemed that the mystery of Christopher's death was to remain for ever a mystery. Jepson had been subjected to a further examination by the authorities; but the case, which had started off with a violent outcry against the perpetrator of such a bestial outrage, gradually fell away from the public interest and in time it was all but forgotten.

And the only good result of the whole ghastly business—an insignificant trifle!—was that the lessee of the building in Jermyn Street was compelled to fix burglar-bars to the windows.

One bright morning in late April I was strolling through the Park when I was accosted by a voice that made me wheel round sharply.

I had been thinking of Sylvia (it was seldom nowadays that she was far from my thoughts) and was trying to decide whether it was now time to make the inevitable proposal to her. I had little doubt about what her answer would be. I had hitherto refrained from forcing myself upon her out of respect for Christopher's memory; but six months is a long time in the lives of young people, and I had judged that she would not take my advances amiss. I had been seeing her almost daily during the winter—except for two months while she was abroad with Lady Somerton—and I knew that of the many young men of her acquaintance I was the one who stood first in her favour. But it would not do to delay too long or I might find someone stepping in before me. Young Sydney Wetherhouse, for instance—Professor Wetherhouse's son, a shy young boy just lately down from Oxford—I could see by his manner that he was completely infatuated by Sylvia's beauty and that at any time his infatuation might even get the better of his extreme shyness.

"Hello, old chappie!" exclaimed the voice that made me wheel round so sharply. "And how the devil are you?"

It was my cousin Mick.

I did not answer for a moment. I could only stare in consternation, while he overtook me with all his old blatant swagger, looking me up and down meanwhile with smiling, insolent freedom.

This was the cousin who was now in possession of the family estates.

"And how is old Makepeace?" my cousin went on, falling into step beside me, his hands stuck easily into the trouser pockets of his light tweed suit. "Still scratching about trying to make ends meet? It was a bitter blow for Makepeace," he went on, "when I booted him out. Almost as bitter as for you, my dear cousin Martin."

Two years—for it was two years since I had seen Mick—had done nothing to abate his unreasonable hatred of me, a hatred that had survived since our childhood days and that had always been shown by semi-humorous, condescending taunts.

"You see where virtue leads," he continued. "You remember all those old women—Makepeace included—who used to ask me why I couldn't be nice and polite—like dear little Martin. And why I didn't sit on the edge of the chair and speak when I was spoken to—like dear little Martin. And why I didn't go to Sunday school—like dear little Martin. And why I wasn't a damned little hypocrite—like dear little Martin . . . But how are you, anyway? You look moderately flourishing. I will admit. Probably you've had a good bit of experience in the art of making a little go a long way."

I ought to have turned and walked away from him; but such a gesture would have been lost on Mick. He would simply turn and walk away along with me. He had a queer sense of fun, and it had always given him immense pleasure to amuse himself at my expense. I found it best to say as little as possible.

"What are you doing these days?" I asked.

"Spending money," he replied. "But the savour has somehow gone out of life for me."

"Oh! How is that?"

"Well, you see, when the family fortune, which we all thought to be yours, turned out to be not yours at all but mine, I was able to pay off all my debts. That left a blank in my existence—a hollowness, a real sorrow. I began to droop. I couldn't feel the zest for things which I had felt previously. And the worst of it is that I can't recover the fine old rapture. I keep on spending, but I can't get into debt at all, at all."

"It should be easy enough," I remarked, smiling.

"Oh, I've no doubt I'll manage it in time," he said with the utmost seriousness. "You come after me, don't you? I mean in the matter of the fortune. On my decease, you know. The cold, pallid corpse business. When I'm laid to rest you come into the fortune. That's something pleasant to reflect upon. But I shouldn't reflect too hopefully, if I were you. There mightn't be any fortune to come into. The last years of my life might be brightened by the thought that I have at last managed to get into debt. No, I shouldn't reflect too hopefully."

As we strolled along I, too, put my hands in my trouser pockets, and thereby did my best to show that I was in no whit disconcerted by his whimsical taunts.

"So you aren't married yet?" I asked.

"No," said he. Then he stopped in his saunter and looked at me quizzically. I knew that some further whimsicality was coming. "But thanks for the reminder," he said. "Of course you are interested in whether I am married or not. Should I marry and have children it will completely put the lid on your expectations. Why didn't I think of that by myself? . . . I told you just now not to reflect too hopefully. I tell you now not to reflect at all. I'm going to marry the first pretty girl 1 see."

I laughed companionably. He vastly exaggerated my interest in his fortune. He was welcome to it, for my tastes were simple and I had enough for my needs. I had not, at that time, considered how much I should want in order to maintain Sylvia in the comfort to which she was apparently accustomed.

"And the first pretty girl you see," I remarked, "might run you into debt and so brighten things up for you long before the last years of your life."

"Well said, dear cousin Martin!" he exclaimed. "Really, you are making some valuable suggestions this morning. You are becoming quite brilliant and worldly. I am quite beginning to take to you . . . And while we are on the subject of your development—

emergence from the nursery stage, you know—what's all this I've been hearing about you and the celebrated Miss Vernon?"

I started at that; and my attempt at sang-froid was in danger of falling to pieces. I knew that my cousin's semi-humorous manner sprang from a very real bitterness towards me. It was quite true that in our very young days I was held up as a paragon of docility and correct behaviour, and though I had long since outgrown that, Mick had never forgotten. And I knew that out of sheer love of discomfiting me he would recklessly destroy anything that I had set my heart upon.

"And what have you been hearing," I asked, "about the celebrated Miss Vernon and me? Is she very celebrated, by the way?"

"Is she! Rather! I'm told that royalty is interested in her. But that's probably an exaggeration. Anyway, I should like to congratulate you."

"You've nothing to congratulate me upon," I assured him, trying, for my own protection, to make as little of the matter as possible.

"Cut out the humility!" he said, with a touch of genuine impatience. "I know all about you and Miss Vernon. The two of you are only waiting for a decent time to elapse after the murder of that young fellow Knight so that you can be married. Has it ever occurred to you to ask yourself how the dickens you're going to maintain her? Not that it's any business of mine, you understand."

"The question," I replied, still trying to turn his mind away from the matter of Sylvia, "is whether I am going to maintain her at all. That depends on two things: firstly, on whether I intend to ask her to allow me to maintain her; and, secondly, on what she might say should I ask her. I haven't considered the question. You seem to know a lot more about me than I know myself."

"Of course I do! Always did! And it worries me to think of the way the two of you will have to scrape and screw to keep up an appearance. She has no money of her own, I'm told. That fact has put quite a number of blue-blooded but penurious youths out of court. But it doesn't deter you, who have never been noted for your sagacity. And—might I add?—it doesn't deter me. I told you that my income grows faster than I can spend it."

I laughed, trying hard not to take him seriously; but I could not keep my uneasiness at bay.

"You are welcome to enter the lists with all the others, I suppose," I commented, "and have a shot at winning the hand of the lady."

"Of course I am," he seconded. "More than that, it is my duty to enter the lists. I must try to save the lady from the horror of a descent from a Park Lane mansion to a flat in the Brompton Road —a flat run by old Makepeace . . . And I told you," he went on, gazing ahead of him with a queer expression of sudden satisfaction on his face, "that, on your suggestion, I should marry the first pretty girl I met. Here she is."

I, too, looked up. Not fifty paces away, coming towards us at an easy walk, was Sylvia.

I had known that she was in the Park. They had told me so when I called at the house less than an hour earlier, and I had been strolling about in the expectation of meeting her. But I had not reckoned on Mick's appearing, and I would have given much to be able to avoid her. But that was now impossible.

Mick's jaunty satisfaction on that occasion strikes me now as infinitely pathetic. Mick's happiness was secure in the promise of being able to shoulder me out of the way. It never occurred to him that he was taking the first step in another tragedy. Of course it didn't. Such a thought never occurred even to me.

"The irony of it!" he whispered. "To think that you must introduce me! For you must, you know, Martin. You can't very well avoid it."

And I introduced them.

Sylvia flushed as she looked up at this debonair cousin of mine.

"I could tell at once that you were related," she said as we turned and fell into step, one on either side of her.

"Am I so very like Martin?" asked Mick. "Thanks for the compliment, Miss Vernon. That's one of the few things our family has been noted for—the persistence of the family likeness. Even Mad Roderick had it."

"And who was Mad Roderick?"

"Mad Roderick—*circa* 1600: that's all I know," Mick replied. "His portrait is in the family gallery. Remember how I used to frighten you, Martin, by trying to pull a face like Mad Roderick's? . . . By the way, I saw you in Rome about a month ago, Miss Vernon."

This remark surprised me, and I was not sure whether my cousin were telling the truth or whether he had accidentally heard that Sylvia had been in Rome.

"Where?" she asked, deliciously intrigued. "What was I doing?"

"It was in the Piazza di something-or-other. You were just walking past."

"And you knew me?"

She had frailties. She turned her head and glanced up into his face, and when her eyes almost immediately sought the path again she was smiling and blushing at the same time.

"I didn't," he said. "But I took the liberty of finding out who you were. You'll forgive me, I'm sure."

"I don't know whether I shall. It *was* a liberty, as you admit."

"Call it rather compulsory curiosity," he replied.

As for me, I was quite out of it, and I strolled along feeling very sheepish and raw. I prided myself on having some skill at conversation of this sort, but, compared with my cousin, I was a mere ploughboy.

"You never told me, Martin," said Sylvia, "that you had a cousin in London."

"I didn't know. I met Mick only half an hour ago—for the first time in two years."

"Were you looking for me?"

"I was mooning about—yes."

"Well, you must both come in and have lunch. It will be about on the table by the time we get back. You must have a great deal to say to each other after such a long time."

Needless to say, Mick accepted. Had I had my wits about me I should have said that I had an appointment elsewhere, and Sylvia could hardly then take my cousin home alone. But I missed the opportunity.

Not that it would have mattered, for I see now that events would have gone on their inevitable course notwithstanding every puny human effort to divert them.

Still abreast we left the Park by the Grosvenor Gate, and in a moment or two were going up the marble steps towards the hall of the mansion that I now knew so well.

But the honours of the occasion lay with my cousin. It was he who was doing the talking, and he was keeping Sylvia amused with so much ease and freedom that one would think he had known her for years.

I was intensely depressed and out of humour.

CHAPTER V

A QUEER BEDROOM

WHEN LUNCH was over, my cousin insisted upon taking me to see his new flat up near Baker Street.

He had, he told us, absorbed the ideas of half a dozen nations during his travels, and at the moment his flat was his hobby and he ventured to believe that it was unique.

He spoke with the pride of the connoisseur, and, with Sylvia sitting there, I could not be so ungracious as to tell him that I was not in the least bit interested in his flat. Sylvia had no suspicion of the intense animosity that existed between my cousin and me.

His manner towards me had changed since the meeting with Sylvia. An observer might have thought that he and I were on the friendliest possible terms, and the way in which he put his hand on my shoulder as he went down the steps towards Park Lane might have misled anybody.

But I was not deceived. At this early stage of his acquaintance-ship with Sylvia I would be useful to him. He could only keep in touch with her through me. But I went with him. I did not want to antagonize him further at the moment, for I had made up my mind to put the inevitable question to Sylvia at the very first opportunity, and I did not want to disturb the position in the meantime.

Mick's flat was all that he had stated it to be. I saw at once that his fortune must be enormous, and that he must, as he had whimsically said, be doing his best to run through it.

The flat was on the top floor of the building. The top-floor flats were small and airy and the bottom-floor flats were large and close; so, he told me, he had conceived the idea of having two top-floor flats converted into one and thus obtaining a place that was large and that was, at the same time, exposed to such invigorating air as London could provide. He had heard, he said, that a factory with a tall chimney was about to be erected on a waste piece of ground near at hand. If there were any truth in the rumour, which he doubted, he would, he said, buy up the factory immediately on its completion and have it demolished again. This, as he pointed out with the extremely serious expression that accompanied his most facetious ideas, would be a splendid way of getting rid of quite a lot of money.

"So you go in for fresh air nowadays?" I questioned.

He had already shown me one or two of the rooms, and was probably thinking that I was feeling envious because of the evidence everywhere of his extreme wealth.

"Yes," he said. "I acquired the taste for fresh air when I was in Australia. Come and see my bedroom. It is, I think, the only one of its kind in London."

When I saw the bedroom I agreed with him.

It seemed that he had had the whole of the outer wall knocked down and rebuilt a good eight or ten feet within the room, thus leaving a good-sized verandah kind of place almost wholly exposed to the weather. In this out-door room stood a camp-bed.

"Those who don't think I am mad," he said as we entered this unique bedroom, "think I am a confirmed invalid of some sort. You see that part of this room is actually the gallery that the tradesmen use. At first it disconcerted them, but I have now arranged with the milkman to give me a nudge when he passes in the morning. A shilling a week that costs me. It goes a very small way towards demolishing my fortune, but it keeps him from expressing his opinions on my sanity."

I laughed. Mick could be very agreeable and amusing when it suited him.

"And you have a good view from here," I said, walking forward to the iron railing of the gallery and looking across towards the parks. "I didn't know there was such a mass of trees in London."

"Oh, a splendid view!" he agreed. "And some day, if money can perform the miracle, I'm going to have a tree planted down there."

He looked over the railing at the concrete courtyard, a hundred feet below.

I, too, looked, instinctively drawing back as I did so.

Galleries similar to the one we were on ran at intervals across the building, getting smaller and less easily discernible as the eye travelled downwards—and, at the bottom, the courtyard, with a clearly defined but diminutive woman washing out a bucket with a mop near what seemed to be a drain. The bucket slipped from the woman's hand and rolled over, and it had ceased to roll before the sharp clatter of galvanized metal ascended faintly to our ears.

"You see," said my cousin, leaning heavily on the rail, "concrete is so uninspiring. That's why I want a tree."

He took me indoors again and showed me his books and kept me interested until tea-time. He was refraining admirably from his habit of being maliciously humorous at my expense. In fact, I was almost deceived by his manner and was inclined to think that his startling threats about whisking Sylvia right from under my eyes had been made merely to tease and annoy me.

But he could not for long resist the temptation to show the contempt in which he held me.

"You like the place?" he asked as he was bidding me good-bye.

I said I did—immensely. And he went on:

"Fit for a princess, don't you think? Fit, even, for Miss Vernon, eh? It was a toss-up between this one and a poky little place in the Brompton Road. I hadn't then made up my mind whether I wanted merely a place to sleep in or whether I wanted a real home. I chose this. I'm glad now that I did. Miss Vernon will like it. I'm sure she'll like it. I must try to induce her and Lady Somerton to pay me a visit. It could be done, I think. The novelty of the place will be a sufficient excuse . . . By the way, did I tell you that Lady Somerton asked me whether I would have a chair in her box at the theatre to-morrow night?"

"No," I said, turning towards him as the elevator began to move up from far down in the well that yawned beside us. "Did she ask you?"

"Yes. At lunch time. And Miss Vernon will be there, of course. I understood that you were going too."

"I am."

"That's good!" he exclaimed, as the elevator cage stopped in front of us and I slipped the trellised gate aside. "You will be able to amuse Lady Somerton during the intervals."

I was lost for a response. I have already said that I was no match for Mick when it came to the handling of words—nor in any other way, I'm afraid. I did not reply, but let myself down in the elevator and strode out into the street.

And, walking towards the West End, I was conscious of my pitiable insignificance when I compared myself with my cousin. I knew that his intention was to humble me, and I knew that he could succeed. I hated him for his never-dying animosity towards me. Surely I had suffered enough from him in the past! But apparently not. His pleasure in defeating me at every turn was almost diabolical. And, not content with all the harm he had already done, he must try to rob me of Sylvia.

And he would likely succeed. I had held Sylvia's interest—affection, I hoped—through all these months, it is true. But I had had no real opponent. There had been only young Sydney Wetherhouse who could be said to be on intimate terms with Sylvia, and young Wetherhouse was too backward and shy to be regarded seriously.

But Mick had insinuated himself right into the heart of the family within the first half-hour. That was characteristic of him. And he would send my dreams sky-high and take pleasure in doing it—just as he had destroyed my toys in the old days.

But he should not, I asserted to myself. I could bear the loss of anything else, but I could not bear the loss of Sylvia. A kind of instinctive savageness took hold of me, and I swore that nobody should ever rob me of that divine creature.

With the thought of her loveliness I seemed to be filled with superhuman strength and purpose.

I was filled, too, with a supreme confidence that quickened my step and brought a grim smile to my lips. Something seemed to tell me that I had nothing to fear from my cousin, and I laughed condescendingly as I thought of the way in which he had taken me to his magnificent flat with the idea of taunting me with my comparative poverty.

CHAPTER VI

AT THE THEATRE

"SYLVIA," I SAID, nervous now that the supreme moment had arrived, "I want to ask you something."

I don't know why I should have introduced the supreme moment with a speech so unutterably commonplace, but I did.

It was the afternoon of the day following my visit to my cousin's gorgeous flat—the afternoon of the day on which we were all to go to the theatre when I was to amuse Lady Somerton during the intervals.

I had made up my mind that Mick should amuse Lady Somerton during the intervals.

But, despite my self-assurance, I was nervous.

Sylvia and I were alone in a little study kind of a place to the rear of the dining-room. I was conscious of the correctness of my dress, and that helped me a little. I knew, too, that my manner was in keeping with the dignity that surrounded us, and that gave me confidence. But I was conscious most of all of Sylvia's surpassing beauty, and my nervousness sprang from the thought that it could surely be no man's good fortune to have all that loveliness to himself.

She was standing by the fireplace, in which a newly lighted fire flickered brightly and was reflected in the rich and sombre panelling of the room. Though I had known her for six months I had never been able to rise above the feeling that when I was with her I was in the presence of a divine mystery. She was the embodiment of supreme femininity. There was a delicacy and a charm about her that was beyond analysis. Mick had said that royalty was interested in her. He had said that that was probably a rumour, but I could quite believe that it might be true. She had a natural queenliness that made men her slaves whether they would or no.

And this was the girl whom I was about to ask to share my paltry thousand a year.

"What do you want to ask me?" she said, turning her head and looking down into the fire.

My self-assurance vanished then.

I took a step towards her, because now I had to go through with the proposal; but even the correctness of my dress failed to bolster up my courage.

"Sylvia!" I exclaimed, a sudden wave of bravado coming to my aid, "I want you to be my wife. I know I'm not worthy of you," I heard myself adding; "but no man is, and no man could love you more than I do."

Here I took the liberty of putting my hand on her shoulder and turning her half towards me; and I remembered the days—six months ago—when she had been in the habit of linking her arm in mine for spiritual as well as for physical support.

And, remembering that time, I put my other hand under her chin (she was still gazing down into the fire) and tried to raise her face towards mine.

But she slipped from my offered embrace and took a step backwards. And instead of there being on her face an expression of shyness, or confusion, or gladness, there was an undoubted expression of pain.

"Why!" I exclaimed. "I thought—"

"Oh, Martin, I know!" she said. "But I can't answer just now. If only you had asked me a week ago! Or two days ago! . . . Don't make me answer now. Give me some time. Give me until to-night—after the theatre."

I was utterly confounded. For a moment I was speechless. I now realized that I had been certain that her answer would be yes; and my disappointment stunned me.

"But why to-night?" I asked at last. "Or why last week? What has happened in the meantime?"

And before she could answer I realized what had happened.

"No, no!" I went on. "It's wrong of me to ask that. Shall I take you through to Lady Somerton?"

She did not say yes or no; but she turned towards the door, and I fell in beside her.

I knew that, like many another girl, she had caught the charm of my fascinating cousin.

At the door she turned and impulsively clasped my face between her hands and kissed me.

"Oh, Martin!" she sobbed. "You've been so good to me—so good and so patient! If only I knew my own mind!"

With that she was gone, leaving me in the room by myself.

And I was strangely glad.

Knowing that it was only my cousin who stood between me and my complete happiness I felt that I need not worry. I could not for the life of me account for my sudden confidence and elation. But they were there, in the fullest measure.

I left the house without disturbing any of the inmates, and went home to dress for the theatre.

The rendezvous was at the theatre itself. I arrived early, but I took the precaution of asking at the box-office whether Lady Somerton had yet arrived. I gave the number of her box, and the girl who was attending to me—and who proved at close quarters to be less of a girl than she seemed when viewed from the other side of the foyer—rang through on the telephone and ascertained that her ladyship had not arrived.

I thanked her and turned away, and for five minutes or so I paced the parquet floor.

My mind was busy with my cousin. I had not yet hit upon any plan for defeating him in the fight for Sylvia's hand; but I was thinking round the subject and I was confident that I could indeed defeat him.

I had never asserted myself in any of my battles with Mick. It had never been worth it. But with Sylvia Vernon as the stake I knew that I should fight to the last ditch and that I would show a spirit that my self-confident cousin would be amazed to see.

I was hoping that he would arrive before the ladies. A few minutes of private conversation with him might have a wonderful effect.

Then it occurred to me that perhaps he was already here and had gone straight to the box. I did not know what the exact arrangements had been.

For the second time I claimed the attention of the woman whom I had mistaken for a girl, and for the second time she performed strange feats with the telephone on my behalf, and eventually informed me that none of Lady Somerton's party was yet present.

So I strolled about for a further minute or two upon the parquetry, thinking that, after all, it might be as well not to see Mick alone. Family feuds are apt to flare up suddenly into pitched battles.

The interior decorations soon palled on my impatient senses, and I strolled out on to the steps and surveyed Shaftesbury Avenue. Shaftesbury Avenue was lively at that time of the evening.

It would be better, I was thinking, to leave the matter of Mick in the lap of the gods. I had no doubt that there would soon occur an opportunity for my asserting myself, and I should show my cousin how greatly he had under-estimated me all these years.

I kept my eye on the cars and taxis that were drawing up at short intervals at the edge of the kerb, putting down their loads, and sliding off into the traffic stream. And I read all the names over the lighted shops at the opposite side of the street. And I read the row of newspaper placards leaning against a blank wall, and learned that the Budget Surplus was causing the Chancellor of the Exchequer a vast amount of worry, that there had been a West End Tragedy, that there had been an Uproar in the House of Commons, and that Our New Serial was beginning To-day.

Then someone touched my arm, and I found myself looking down into the wistful face of Sylvia.

"Oh, pardon me!" I said. "I was keeping abreast with the news of the day and I didn't see you arrive."

"But where is your cousin?" asked Lady Somerton, putting her head a little on one side and raising her eyebrows in the manner that gave her such an appearance of vivacity. "Are we early?"

"Not too early," I replied. "But he hasn't turned up yet."

I escorted them up the heavily carpeted stairs and along some heavily carpeted corridors.

"He'll know to ask for your box," I remarked, as an attendant opened a door and we found ourselves looking over into a well of humming humanity. "They know you are here. I have already asked for you down in the office."

Sylvia had said nothing except a bare greeting when we met.

The orchestra came to the end of the piece they had been playing when we entered. The conductor fidgeted for a moment with his music and glanced at his watch, apparently uncertain whether to start another piece or not. He did start another piece, but he had not got through many bars when a bell rang, causing him to bring the piece to an early but graceful conclusion.

And still there was no Mick.

"It's very unlike him," I said, mainly to Sylvia; "unless he has altered a lot. He was always on time where a pretty girl was concerned."

I ought not to have said that. It was an unkind thing to say in any case, but it was doubly unkind when he was absent.

But I could not tell what the ladies thought, for the curtain went up then and drew our interest to the stage.

I followed the first few passes of the opening scene, but my mind would wander to the door at our back, and later my eyes followed my mind, and I kept glancing round every now and again, expecting the door to open and Mick to appear in the aperture. Whatever had detained him he would have a story ready, and a few well-chosen words would reinstate him in favour even though it should turn out that he had forgotten all about the appointment.

And from time to time Sylvia also glanced round towards the door.

The first act came to an end, and Lady Somerton turned to me and immediately began to chatter. And she and I chattered throughout the *entr'acte,* while Sylvia, gloomily, I thought, surveyed the auditorium.

The lights went down, and the curtain rose for the second act. But before we could gather what was afoot on the stage, that fascinating door at the back of the box opened and a man—a man who wore dress clothes for the same reason as a commissionaire wears uniform—looked in somewhat furtively.

He beckoned to me noiselessly. I slipped from my chair and joined him at the door. I was not used to being beckoned to by strangers in official dress suits, but there was something about this man's furtive air that aroused immediate curiosity within me.

"You Mr. Martin Strange, sir?" he whispered. I told him that I was.

"There's been a telephone call for you, sir. About your cousin, they said. A Mr. Michael Strange, I think the name was."

"That's right," I said. "We're expecting him here."

"I'm sorry to say that he's dead, sir," said the man, still whispering.

"Dead?"

I stepped out into the dimly lit corridor and pulled the door softly behind me. But it was immediately opened again from the inside, and Sylvia noiselessly joined us.

By the startled expression in her eyes I guessed that she had heard all that had passed. "They've rung off now, sir," went on the man. "They said would you care to go to Green Bay Mansions, Marylebone. I understand that the circumstances are rather—rather tragic."

"What has happened?" asked Sylvia, looking up into my face.

"What exactly did they say?" I asked the man.

At that moment a programme-seller came hurrying along the corridor. She had no programmes, but she had in her hand a hurriedly folded newspaper.

"The manager's compliments," she said to the man, "and perhaps the gentleman would like to read the account in the paper."

She handed me the newspaper as she spoke, pointing with one scarlet-nailed finger to a column headed, "West End Tragedy."

I read through the report, with Sylvia looking over my arm.

"Early this morning," the report ran, "the body of a man, later identified as Michael Strange, a gentleman of independent means who has only recently taken up residence in London, was found lying in the courtyard at the back of Green Bay Mansions, a block of flats in which Mr. Strange lived.

"Mr. Strange had been dead for some hours when the discovery was made.

"Mr. Albert Jones, a milk-roundsman who serves some of the flats, told our representative that he was in the habit of giving Mr. Strange, a young man of about thirty, a call on his first round. Mr. Jones explained that the dead man, who lived on the ninth floor of the building, had had the flat altered so that he might sleep out on the balcony.

"This morning the camp-bed was empty, and had been turned over on its side. Mr. Jones thought this unusual, and happened to look over the rail of the balcony, from which there is a sheer drop of over a hundred feet, and was horrified to see the body of Mr. Strange, clad in pyjamas, lying in the concrete courtyard.

"Mr. Strange has lived almost wholly abroad for the past two years. Three years ago he inherited the fortune of the well-known collector, Abraham Strange, of whom he was a grandson."

I stared at the paper for a long time after I had finished reading the account. Then I saw that Sylvia was looking up at me and that her face had gone a dead white.

We exchanged glances. Rather, we exchanged a long stare.

But I could not guess from her expression whether she were following the same train of thought as I was following.

I was trembling—trembling because I stood on the brink of the unknown; and I was praying that she might not suspect the awful power that I now was certain I possessed. If she knew that, she would flee from me in terror.

It was possible that she was thinking of the coincidence of the tragedy that overtook Christopher Knight and of the tragedy that had now overtaken my cousin—the one a man who had stood between her and me, and the other a man who had threatened to stand between her and me. Long might she continue to think of it only as coincidence!

I leaned heavily against the panelled partition. The programme-seller had vanished; but she now returned, bearing a tray with glasses and a brandy bottle. Chairs had been brought from some-where, and they made Sylvia sit down and made her drink some of the brandy. They made me sit down and drink as well.

They thought that the tragic circumstances of the death of my cousin had upset me. They had. But the death of Mick, terrible though it was, was a small matter compared with the awful truth that some supernatural being was secretly in league with me, ready to destroy anything that stood between me and my desires.

My responsibility was terrifying; and the sense of the nearness of this secret, ghostly presence was unbearable.

CHAPTER VII

SYLVIA'S FEARS

WHEN WE LEFT the theatre (we left it immediately, I believe, though I do not remember leaving it at all) we got into a taxi and drove to Park Lane.

Only Lady Somerton made any effort at conversation; and her observations were such as might be expected to come from a person who saw in the tragedy only the bare fact of a single occurrence. It might have struck her—as I was sure it had struck Sylvia—that to be personally connected with two cases of violent death, happening within six months of each other, makes one uneasy and vaguely superstitious; but she could not guess that both men had stood between me and my desires and that, for that reason, both men were dead.

I tried to attend to what Lady Somerton was saying, and I think I succeeded in concealing my terror from her at least.

But Sylvia was watching me. Many times during the drive I caught her looking at me with wide, horror-stricken eyes—eyes that added to my fear in spite of my trying to assure myself that she could not even suspect the existence of this unearthly power that was so ill-advisedly (if I may use such an expression) working on my behalf.

In Park Lane I assisted them to alight. They expected me to drive straight on then to my cousin's flat; but I could not make up my mind whether to do so or not. The thought of being on the scene of the tragedy filled me with horror. And yet it might look queer if I did not go.

The ladies were going up the steps. I was immediately behind them. I suddenly asked myself, the question springing from nowhere: "Ought I not to give up all thought of Sylvia? My love for her has already caused two deaths: I cannot account for the deaths by any other means. And it might cause other tragedies in the future. Wouldn't it be better—"

At that moment Sylvia turned, leaving Lady Somerton to go on ahead. She stood a step or two above me. The shimmering silver and blue of her opera cloak caught the faint light from the lamps in Park Lane and invested her slim figure with an ethereal and maddening beauty. There was about her the alluring mystery of a goddess.

And I knew it was useless to ask myself whether I ought to give up all thought of her.

"Come in for a moment," she said—rather, she pleaded. "I have something to say—something that I must say."

I inclined my head, wondering, suddenly fearful lest she might have discovered my secret.

I returned to the taxi and paid the driver off, and when I reached the top of the steps the ladies were in the hall and a man-servant was holding the door open for me.

Sylvia disposed of her aunt with a few words that I did not overhear. In the circumstances in which we now found ourselves conventional behaviour was not the greatest thing in the world.

We were once more in the little panelled room at the rear of the house, and once more Sylvia took up a position by the fire, leaning with one hand on the mantelpiece and looking down into the flames. I stood hesitatingly in the middle of the floor, my light overcoat still on, my crush hat and gloves in my hand.

"You asked me a question this afternoon," she said, in a voice so quiet that I could barely catch the words.

"Yes," I murmured, advancing a step in my eagerness.

She turned suddenly and drew away from me.

"Keep away!" she said, intensely excited all at once. "I can't allow you to come near me. Two deaths are enough."

Her words—and especially her manner—repelled me. I concluded, of course, that she had guessed my secret.

"But," I stammered, my mind made up to fight to the very last, "what have the two deaths to do with you and me? I don't understand. You're upset, Sylvia."

And I took another step towards her. Now that I was fighting for the greatest prize in life my own fears had sunk out of sight. My mind was wholly concerned with the business of convincing her that there was nothing abnormal in anything that had happened.

"You are right," she said, taking another step away from me and holding out a hand as though to ward me off. "I am upset, and I don't understand any more than you do. Haven't these two deaths made you think—made you wonder?"

"Now that you mention it, yes," I replied. "It seems unusual that two people whom we know should die in circumstances not normal."

"Haven't you thought more deeply about it than that?"

"No," I lied. "The coincidence certainly struck me."

At all costs I must discourage in her the suspicions that had become certainties with me. My own fears had gone completely. I should have defied hell's legions only so that I might embrace that lovely form.

"And no more than that?" she questioned, going back to the fireplace and leaning again on the mantelpiece. "Didn't you attach any significance to the fact that they were both men—young men? And to the fact that they were both in love—with me?"

"Both in love with you!" I exclaimed. She was getting dangerously near the truth, but what surprised me was the certainty with which she made the statement that they were both in love with her. "But my cousin saw you only once," I added. "How do you know that he was in love with you?"

"How do I know!" She seemed to mock me, and I felt chastened under that faint touch of scorn. "This isn't a time for being reserved about such matters. I know that he was. He told me; but I knew before he told me. I ought to have resented his precipitancy, but I didn't. I felt attracted to him as well. I don't say that I was in love with him. No, no. It was merely that he had a novel personality."

"But you might have fallen in love with him?" I suggested. "That was why you asked me to wait for my answer until after the theatre? You wanted to see whether he improved on a further acquaintance?"

"Something like that," she said, without emotion. "But it doesn't matter now. I repeat that both of these men were in love with me. And they have both died violent deaths."

I could say nothing more that would prevent her from coming to the terrible conclusion towards which she was driving.

"And what do you think that means?" I asked, looking into the fire though my whole attention was on what she was about to say next.

"It means," she said, raising her head and looking at the blank panelled wall in front of her, "that there is a curse upon me . . . You laugh," she added hastily, turning and looking at me with something of anger in her glance, "but it's too serious to be set so easily aside."

I had indeed smiled, or, at least, my face had lighted up with relief at knowing that she did not suspect what I firmly believed to
be the truth of the matter. And now I did really laugh. Even at the
risk of arousing her fully to anger I felt that I must keep her mind
off thoughts of superstition and darkness. "Nonsense!" I exclaimed.

And to dismiss such an idea once and for all I strode swiftly
across to her, and before she had time to draw back I had her in
my arms.

"Forgive me for contradicting you!" I whispered, playfully.
"But it is nonsense, you know. Such things don't happen. Even
Professor Wetherhouse says that he doesn't know of one authenticated instance of ghostly happenings. It's all imagination. You're
upset, as I told you at first."

For a moment she struggled, but I held her firmly.

"Oh, Martin, I'm afraid!" she said, beginning to cry. "I know it
all sounds foolish, but I feel that there are hidden, terrible forces at
work all around me. Uncanny! I feel that people—beings—are
looking at me. It seems—"

"You're thoroughly upset, and that's the short and long of it," I
said lightly. And then my emotion got the upper hand of me and,
without fear of a rebuff, I pressed my lips to hers, fondling her
shoulders and stroking her hair, everything forgotten except the
supreme wonder of her physical closeness.

And she did not attempt to discourage me. Rather, she gave
herself up to my embrace and, with unexpected passion, returned
my kisses. I was in the highest heaven.

Then she drew away from me. I was quite content that she
should, for she was now mine.

But she would return to the old theme. I could only be patient
with her, and I was far *too* happy to be otherwise.

"I can't help saying it, Martin," she murmured, taking my hand
in hers; "but I'm so afraid that something might happen to you
next."

"I'm not—not in the least," I told her lightly. "Why should anything happen to me?"

"Three men have loved me. The other two are dead."

"Only three!" I exclaimed. "Why, there are hundreds who love
you. Nobody can set eyes on you without falling in love with
you."

It was not wise of me to say such a thing, but fortunately she was not a girl readily affected by flattery. She would not think the less of me because everybody else was in love with her.

"But only three whom I have allowed to tell me so," she went on. "I know there are some who want only very little encouragement. But that is what makes me fear for your safety. Two of those who have offered me their love have been killed by—"

"By what? You can't tell me . . . The one by a burglar, perhaps, who was disturbed and flew into a panic. The other—we don't know yet why he should have fallen over the balcony. But it's very certain that ghosts don't exert physical force on people—if that's what you are thinking."

For my own part, I was certain that ghosts did exert physical force on people. The tragedy of my cousin had brought back to me the inevitableness of the circumstances of Christopher Knight's death. And though that might have been merely coincidence, I could not credit that a second death that would benefit me in my wooing of this girl could be other than the work of some conscious power somewhere.

"Ghosts (such a crude term, but you know what I mean!)," went on Sylvia, "might have caused your cousin—through fear or from some kind of suggestion—to throw himself over the balcony."

"But a man couldn't strangle himself with his own hands," I put in, dryly; "and Christopher was strangled."

It seems now that on that night we discussed things with an almost brutal freedom. But the physical fact of death could be spoken of easily and without emotion. There was about us an atmosphere more grim and mysterious than death—an atmosphere of dark foreboding and stealthy terror.

Sylvia had no answer to my last remark except the inconclusive one that something beyond argument made her afraid.

And I could not convince her of the fact that the shock of this second death had unsteadied her nerves.

I could not, I might say, convince myself that her fears were only imaginary. Her suggested explanation had sent my thoughts into fresh avenues of inquiry. That the cause of these tragedies was supernatural I had not the faintest doubt; but I could not guess at the ultimate intention of the power that caused them, nor could I guess at the extent of that power, nor could I guess who might be the victim of its next manifestation. Sylvia might be the next victim, or I might be the next victim.

I was almost trembling again. Man is a puny, defenceless creature in the face of unfathomable mystery—a creature capable only
of terror when threatened by brooding darkness beyond his knowledge.

"I wish I could be as carefree as you," said Sylvia.

I laughed lightly and, putting my arm about her shoulders, led
her to the door. I dared not let her know that my fears were perhaps more intense than her own.

"You will be, to-morrow," I said. "A good night's sleep—that's
all you want."

Yet to the last she remained unconvinced; and when I said good
night, notwithstanding the presence of Lady Somerton who as yet
knew nothing of our declaration of love, she threw her arms about
my neck and kissed me passionately. She did not say, "It might be
your turn to-night!" but I knew that that was what she was thinking.

I went on to Green Bay Mansions, but I made my visit one of
pure duty. For one thing I could do nothing but acknowledge the
valet's goodness in taking the trouble to find me.

I did not look at the body. I mumbled some excuse—I *forget*
what I said—and left again as quickly as I could. To see that bedroom again, and to be near that gallery with its perspective of galleries almost vanishing down by that concrete courtyard, would
have filled me with horror.

My only chance of mental peace lay in not encouraging morbid
thoughts—in deliberately refusing to think of all that might lie
behind these two deaths.

In the busy streets again, where innocent life was in full swing,
the happiness of my few rapturous moments with Sylvia came
back to me—if it had ever left me—and the world was once more
a place of joy and promise. Contact with my fellows made fear
stand aside for a while. Morbid thoughts could go to the devil. The
great fact was Sylvia's acceptance of my love.

I strode off towards Oxford Street with the intention of finding
a taxi to take me home to my dingy rooms in the Brompton Road.

Then I realized that all my cousin's wealth was now mine. I
hadn't thought of that until that moment.

CHAPTER VIII

A VOICE FROM THE PAST

DESPITE THE EASE with which I had consigned all morbid thoughts to the place from whence they come, I had no sooner put my latch-key into the door of my flat than I became conscious of dark forebodings.

I did not immediately open the door. I stood for an instant with my key in the lock, thinking.

What if Sylvia were right? I pictured the dark hall beyond this solid door (Makepeace was very niggardly on my behalf and resolutely refused to keep the hall light switched on unless somebody were going out or coming in), and I pictured my dark bedroom and I thought of the many hours between now and daybreak. And I remembered that Makepeace was growing deaf, and that, in any case, he was too old and feeble to be of any use in an emergency.

Shame made me muster up my courage, and I turned the key and threw the door wide.

The hall light, surprisingly, was blazing away heedless of expense; and as I shut the door behind me, the grizzled old Makepeace appeared from his own domain and came towards me, I thought, in quite a sprightly fashion.

"Did they find you, sir?" he asked eagerly.

"You mean about Mick? . . . Yes. You know that he's gone?"

"Ah! They told me—when they telephoned to ask how they could get into touch with you. I was hoping—I was hoping that they might not find you, sir. I should have liked to be the one to tell you the news."

This curious statement puzzled me, but I did not question it. While Makepeace was taking my hat and coat I contented myself with remarking, "Yes, he's gone. Rather tragic!"

The last thing I wanted was to have to discuss the affair.

"Tragic in a way," conceded the old man. "But he was a wild one, if I might take the liberty of saying so, who knew his grandfather."

"You know how he died, I suppose. Did they tell you that?"

Averse though I was to speaking about the matter, I was forced
to offer to give Makepeace the essential particulars.

"Yes," said Makepeace. "He died the same way as his grandfather died—him that I just mentioned—his grandfather on his
mother's side, that is to say."

I had been about to step forward to go to the sitting-room with
the intention of reading for an hour or so before turning in, but the
old man's words arrested me.

"Oh!" I said. "That's curious."

"Yes, you might well say that, sir. And they never got at the
rights of the case."

"They didn't? Why, what happened? Funny that I've never
heard anything about this!"

"Not funny, Mister Martin. The case was hushed up as far as
might be. There were too many queer rumours going about. It was
best not to say too much—especially to them as were interested, as
you might say."

"Interested?"

"Yes. The family, you know. There was enough strife without
adding to it. The Strange family have always been a lot for going
at it hammer and tongs with each other."

"Would you care to tell me about it?" I asked, signing to the
old man to precede me into the sitting-room.

Here was something, I thought, that might help me at this time,
when my mind was groping vaguely in darkness. It had never occurred to me to ask Makepeace whether there were any matters to
be learned in the family history.

"Well, seeing as you're the only one left, Mister Martin, and
you've no one to quarrel with and there's no one to quarrel with
you, I don't see why you shouldn't know. You can't quarrel with
your- self—though I don't know about that, even. There's some
people who—"

Makepeace was perfectly willing to speak about matters that he
had kept faithfully hidden throughout generations; but he was not
willing to precede me into the sitting-room. He insisted on my going first, while he took the door out of my hand and held it open
and stood stiffly until I passed him.

I could very well have turned to him and said, "Why do you
humble yourself before me, Mr. Makepeace? It's I who ought to
hold the door for you. You have a greater right to my respect than
I have to yours. Can I equal you in any of the things that matter—

in fidelity, in experience, in wisdom, in a hundred other things by which the worth of a man is judged?"

But I didn't speak. For one thing, he was not humbling himself before me.

He was good enough to take a seat. Had he been only a few years younger, I think he would have insisted upon standing throughout the interview.

"When I heard the news, Mister Martin, I said to myself that it was his grandfather all over again. And so it is, and you mark my words—they'll never get to the bottom of it."

"But the inquest hasn't been held yet."

"That may be. But a hundred inquests won't bring them a step farther forward. I don't say that because it's Mister Michael. I say it because there'll be nobody to swear whether it was murder or whether it was suicide or whether it was misadventure—walking in his sleep, for instance. I know, because that was the difficulty with his grandfather. There was nothing to show one way or the other what had happened. They said it was misadventure."

"What grounds had they for saying that?"

"No grounds whatever. Or, if you like, the grounds of Christianity. They couldn't say anything else very well, if you understand me."

"No; of course not," I admitted.

"No more will they be able to say anything else in this case . . . Only with his grandfather's death there was a difference. And that was what all the talk was about at the time, and it was a great pity that a word was spoken, though I kept my mouth shut and maybe I had more right to speak than some that had the most to say."

"Will you have something to drink?" I interrupted, asking the question not because I thought there was the least likelihood of his accepting, but because I was curiously thrilled by his manner and felt the need of something to steady my pulses. Makepeace had suddenly been transformed from the old servant—"scratching about trying to make ends meet," as my cousin had put it only the day before—into a voice from the dead past.

"If the liberty will be excused," he said. "This is a great day, Mister Martin; and if it weren't for the fact that a young soul has been cut off suddenly, I would—"

He did not finish the sentence, but I knew what he wanted to say. He wanted to say that he would throw his hat into the air and dance a jig.

And at the same time I understood what he had meant when he said, on my first coming into the flat that night, that he had hoped to be the one to tell me the news. And I understood the meaning of the lighted hall. To Makepeace the affairs of my family were the breath of life; and the fact that I had come into the whole of the estates and fortune was to him, who had watched disputes being carried on through generations, enough to make this a day among days, a day when history was being made, a day for unrestrained rejoicing—even a day on which he might drink with the master.

I went to the sideboard (my sitting-room and dining-room were one and the same) and brought forward a tray. Makepeace was for doing this, but I made him keep his seat.

Nevertheless, he did stand up—with a glass in his hand.

"To the Family!" he said, in rather a shaky voice. "To the return of its glory, and to the end of strife!"

We clinked glasses.

At first I was conscious of a feeling of awkwardness, as though this were a pretty piece of sentimental make-believe that I would be ashamed to be caught in. But my old servant's moist eyes and his voice that was shaky with emotion and sincerity caught me all of a sudden; and when I had drunk I set down my glass and clasped his hand in both of mine.

And after a while, when we were seated again, I told him that I had, that very day, become unofficially engaged to Miss Sylvia Vernon. And he knew all about Miss Sylvia Vernon, though he had never set eyes upon her—that is to say, he knew who her parents were, and who her uncles and aunts were, and in what distant way she was related to this nobleman and the other nobleman, and so on.

His congratulation occupied a good few minutes.

"And the family of Strange," he concluded, "will fairly come back to its old glory . . . You'll have sons—Heaven grant that you may have sons!—so that there'll never be lacking an heir. And as you're making such a fair start of it—building up a new family, as you might say—maybe you'll lay the ghost as well."

"Lay the ghost!" I echoed, suddenly brought back to the affairs of the moment.

"Well, well!" he said, with, I thought, a glint of amusement in his eye. "There's been talk of a ghost; but there's hardly a family of any age that hasn't had a ghost of some sort, if you believe all you hear. And the family of Strange have certainly had enough trouble one way and another to make anybody think they had more than one ghost stumping about. . .. But I was speaking about Mister Michael's grandfather—Sir Osmond Garway."

I settled myself to listen, and as the recital proceeded I became more and more intensely interested, for I began to suspect that the facts had a very direct bearing on my own experiences.

"When I was a lad," Makepeace went on, "I went into your family's service. (I'm speaking of sixty to sixty-five years ago.) Your grandfather, Abraham Strange, was the head of the house then. He was a young man, about your own age—maybe a bit older—and he and his mother lived, of course, in Hampshire, at Bolton Towers. Now Abraham had a friend, this Sir Osmond Garway, that he had picked up at college. Though why he wanted to pick up such a thoroughgoing bad lot I could never fathom, for Abraham, your grandfather, was one of the quietest men I ever seen—always reading, he was, and studying and what not.

"Anyway, young Sir Osmond was often down at Bolton Towers, and the two of them seemed to hit it off uncommonly well, all things considered. It was when the girl came on the scene that things began to shape somewhat different.

"This girl was called Cecilia, and a regular highflyer *she* was. Abraham brought her along—I don't know where he found her; but before very long she was a regular visitor. And everybody, of course, thought that she was to be the mistress of Bolton Towers, though she wasn't the sort that you would expect Abraham to marry—any more than you would think Abraham would make a friend of Sir Osmond. But there you are.

"Well, he didn't marry her. Sir Osmond married her, which was more in keeping, as you might say. But it hurt Abraham, I know that, for she was a pretty slip of a thing for all her high-flying ways and her rampageous temper.

"Sir Osmond and his lady used to come about the place pretty much as before, and Abraham never gave a sign but what he was perfectly satisfied with the way things had panned out.

"Then *he* got married—Abraham, I mean. And everybody thought that it was as well that he had waited, for the girl he picked was exactly the girl you would imagine would suit him— and so she did and she made him a good wife.

"And in the meantime Sir Osmond and Lady Garway weren't hitting it off none too grand. And Lady Garway had a daughter, when Sir Osmond wanted a son, and they had a row over that—as though such things aren't in the hands of Providence. But it was only that they had got out of patience with each other, and there's no reasonableness when people are out of patience with each other.

"Well, the upshot of that was that Lady Garway took it into her head to live abroad for the best part of the year, and Sir Osmond used to come down to Bolton Towers for week-ends just as he used to do in the old days before Cecilia came on the scene.

"But Abraham, even though he had such a wonderfully pleasant wife, used to spend the most of his time in the library; and so it came about that Sir Osmond—that crawling snake in the grass—began to take particular notice of the mistress. And then the thing happened.

"I might never have known anything about it—and I would have had a happier life if I hadn't—but for one of the tenants calling one evening after the dinner was over. This tenant wanted to see the master about something or other and wouldn't be put off. He was the dangdest determined fellow you ever see, by name Marston, but that's got nothing to do with it, except that to keep the man quiet I went to tell the master.

"I couldn't find the master. But this Marston fellow said that I must find the master and that he wouldn't move from those front steps until I did find him. So off I went again, and I searched all the inside of the house; and when I found that he wasn't in any of the public rooms and wasn't in his own suite, I started on the outside, for it was a middling fine night, I remember, and I thought as maybe the master was having a stroll about the grounds.

"And sure enough I did come across him, down yonder by the shrubbery—where you, sir, and Mister Michael and that redheaded rascal of the steward's used to play cricket and quarrel all the time. It was there, under the trees, that I found him—him and Sir Osmond, as I could see by the moon's light.

"I was going a step at a time along the edge of the lawn, wondering whether I ought to worry him or not; and when I got close enough I could hear that the two of them were having high words. I stopped and turned tail, thinking to myself that Marston could go hang and wait on the steps for the rest of the night if he felt like it. *I* wasn't going to risk being sworn at for none of the tenants, however urgent their business might be.

"But I didn't go far. I'm as curious as the next one about other folk's affairs, and I could hear that the words were flying pretty thick. So I stopped and crept back, and got by the end of that clump of rhododendrons by the wall of the orchard. You know where I mean. It was the same then as it is now.

"I heard Sir Osmond say, 'Oh, ho! So you think I kissed her, do you? Perhaps *she* told you that! You wouldn't care to admit that *she* told you that?'

"Abraham didn't answer for a minute, and I could see that Sir Osmond was strutting about as though he had said something that had fairly stumped the master. Then he stopped his strutting about and leaned against a tree, as careless as you like, so that I myself, though I didn't know anything about it, could have stepped out and knocked him down.

" 'So, so!' says he. 'You can't say that it was she who told you, which means that it was somebody else. It's wrong of you to listen to tales, Abraham,' he says, 'especially to tales that don't do credit to your own wife. Must *I* teach you the rules of common trustfulness?' he says with a sneer. 'Don't you think your wife would have told you if I had attempted to kiss her? And why ask me to leave this charming place because of a mere rumour?'

"I saw the master take a step towards his one-time friend; and Sir Osmond straightened himself—I thought, rather quickly. 'Nobody told me,' cried the master. 'I saw you with my own eyes—out here, before dinner. I know what I'm talking about,' he says, 'and I tell you to leave here to-night.'

" 'But you mustn't say such things,' said the other fellow, beginning again with his strutting about. 'Think of the position. What will people say?'

" 'I don't care what they say,' says the master.

"Then Sir Osmond stopped. He was smiling now, so far as I could make out.

" 'Shall I tell you what they'll say?' he asked. 'They'll say that the young fellow Strange is making a sad fist at it—that he lost his first sweetheart and now he's nearly lost his first wife.'

"At that the master fairly flew at him, and if his fist had landed where it was meant to land, Sir Osmond wouldn't have had much to say for the rest of *that* night. But the master hadn't any skill in that line, and all he did was to swing himself off his balance and send himself sprawling.

"I was ready then to run out and help him, but Sir Osmond simply stood still and watched the master pick himself up, and then he turned and walked towards the house. And in a minute the master followed him, running a few steps and then stopping, as though he wasn't quite sure what to do.

"Nothing more was said that I could hear, and they both went into the house through the conservatory. And when I went into the drawing-room a few minutes later to say that this tenant fellow was waiting on the doorstep, the two of them were with the other guests and acting as if nothing had happened.

"That night Sir Osmond Garway was killed.

"His room was in the West Tower, just over the study—sixty feet up, as near as you might judge; and in the morning they found him lying on the gravel just outside the big dining-room. And to this day nobody knows what happened.

"There were stories going about, of course. Some said it was suicide on account of his wife being such a tartar, and some said that he must have been walking in his sleep and that his window happened to be wide open because of the mild weather and that he had scrambled through it in mistake. And it came out then that quite a lot of folks suspected something about his goings on with the master's wife, and put two and two together.

"But I'm as sure that the master had nothing to do with it as I'm sure that there's a God in heaven, for I knew the master as well as I knew myself, and he couldn't do such a thing.

"He was real upset over it. He broke down before me the next day and cried like a baby. 'Makepeace,' says he, 'I hated that man. May God forgive me I If I had known that this would happen maybe I should have had greater charity towards him.'

"I remember the very words, and I remember the way he cried. And I knew, anyway, that there was no evil in the master. But it wasn't everybody who knew him as well as I knew him, and a heap was said that needn't have been said.

"I never told a soul what I had heard; but now that you're the master—"

The rest of Makepeace's words trailed away out of my consciousness. I could see that he was still speaking, because his lips were moving and his expression was changing with the current of his thoughts, but of what he was saying I knew nothing.

Then his expression became strangely fixed. He was looking steadily at me.

"What's the matter, sir?" I heard him say then, and I saw him rise to his feet and come towards me.

"Nothing!" I protested, jumping up at the same time.

But almost immediately I collapsed into my chair again and sat, I suppose, dazedly, while Makepeace fussed about me.

My former periods of horror had been nothing to this. I had given to tragic events a grim enough significance, in all conscience, but at the back of my mind there had always existed a desire to account for the mysterious deaths by purely material explanations. I had tried to tell myself that coincidence might have played a large part in the affairs, that Christopher Knight might have been murdered by a panic-stricken burglar, and that my cousin had suddenly become insane and jumped to his death. And though these explanations did not in the least satisfy me—for feeling as well as reason made me look for explanations deeper than these—they were nevertheless present, and afforded some promise of escape from sheer insane horror. But Makepeace's story destroyed once and for all any hope that I might ever have had of the relief that a commonplace elucidation of the mysteries would have brought me. The power that was active in my case was the same—I could not doubt it—as the power that had destroyed the enemy of my ancestor, Abraham Strange.

I told Makepeace just what had happened. He, of all men, was the safest confidant I could have. I told him about Christopher, and how I had desired his death for the few moments when I was under the influence of overwhelming jealousy, and how the death had taken place that same night. And I told him about Mick, and how he had taunted me and threatened to steal Sylvia, and how *he* had died the same night.

And the face of Makepeace grew whiter and whiter; and when I had finished and was sitting with my head in my hands, trying to grasp the fearful extent of all this, and wondering, I suppose, why I should be singled out from my fellows and set apart into a world of dark mystery, Makepeace came over and put his hand on my shoulder, his fingers clutching me and working nervously the while.

"Then it's true!" he said, half to himself. "May God have mercy on us!"

"What is true?" I asked, looking up.

"The curse, or the ghost, or whatever it is that has caused so many queer things to happen in the family's history. I used to think they were only old stories, but . . ."

Looking back on that night I wonder how I had the courage to go to bed. But I did go to bed eventually, compromising with my feelings by keeping the light in my bedroom burning all night. Yet even that did little to soothe my intensely sensitive imagination, and I lay awake for hours, reading in every slightest creak of a board the immediate manifestation of some lurking unseen presence.

Morning found me unrefreshed; and it was morning, with its mock relief of daylight, that made me realize that I should never be free of this haunting terror. Sixty years ago, and six months ago, and two days ago the power had asserted itself. It might spring again to-night or in twenty years' time. I could never tell. And never being able to tell was, I thought, the most refined kind of mental torture.

But why should *I* be terror-stricken? I asked myself the question when I was in the midst of dressing and when the morning sun and the sounds of human activity had indeed pushed back the terrors of the night, I was almost a normal reasoning being again. At any rate, I was able to recollect that the unseen forces were working in my favour and that had nothing to be afraid of.

Pitiful attempt at self-deceit! As though the fact that my thoughts were being read by a ghostly presence was nothing to be afraid of!

CHAPTER IX

A SUSPECT

IT WAS TWO or three mornings later that I found myself walking across the Park towards Lady Somerton's residence.

I had taken to walking wherever I wanted to go. The uneasiness of my mind seemed to be relieved by exercise, and to tire myself out physically was the only way by which I could then ensure myself a night's sleep. And even in those few days I was already benefiting from the unusual exercise: my thoughts were less morbid, and there was less of that atmosphere of horror with which my mind had invested even the common things of life.

And I thought: "It is a question of not dwelling upon the significance of all that has happened. A healthy body predisposes towards a healthy mind. How much greater will be the effect of the exercise of a strong will! My fears spring from my thoughts, and my thoughts are subject to my will. I can force myself to set morbid thoughts aside."

It was then that I met the Professor.

He was coming over, he said, to see me. I told him that I was honoured, then he went on:

"I haven't seen you since your cousin died, and I wanted to offer my sympathy. An ordinary death in a family is bad enough, but tragedy makes it so much worse. Were you surprised at the verdict?"

The Professor's question took me on the hop. The truth was that I had not made myself acquainted with the result of the inquest. My mind had been so fully engaged on matters that were far beyond the scope of coroners that I had not even thought about the inquest. The inquest had been to me merely a formal affair, as the funeral would be merely a formal affair. It could have no bearing on the real cause that lay behind the death.

"No," I said, ashamed of my ignorance and hoping to be able to cover it up, for no one who did not know the truth but would think it inhumanly callous of me not even to buy a newspaper to see what had happened. The fact was that I had not seen a newspaper for days. "But it's very good of you, Professor," I went on hurriedly, "to think of coming over to see me. I appreciate it very much."

I could see that he was looking at me out of the corner of his eye, and that made me uncomfortable. I wondered whether I had handled the situation so awkwardly as to make him suspect that I had never once thought about the inquest. But that, I argued, was impossible.

Yet, as we walked along the path towards Park Lane—at a gentle pace, for the Professor was past the violently active part of his life—he continued to look at me, as I thought, stealthily, from time to time.

"The worst of it is," he remarked, "that there isn't the unanimity that one hopes for in a case of this sort. The verdict is plain enough, of course—misadventure. But—"

I was relieved to hear that the verdict was in accordance with my expectations. I could now talk more freely to the Professor.

"But," he went on, "when you read between the lines you see that there was some doubt in the mind of the court. But you were there, of course, and you had a better chance of forming an opinion than I who only saw the report in the newspaper. What did you think?"

"I wasn't there," I said, with an effort at frankness, though conscious again of his sidelong, stealthy glance. "I couldn't face the ordeal. I've known Mick since he was a boy. That might seem to you, sir, to be all the more reason why I should be present on such an occasion. But the reverse is the case. I couldn't face it."

I was surprised at the ease with which I told that lie. It was a small matter. It was no business of the Professor's whether I was at the inquest or not. I might quite readily have told him that I had no particular love for my cousin in life and that I was not one to indulge in spurious sentimentality because my cousin was no longer alive. But I dissembled. Something made me wish to hide the truth.

The Professor seemed to swallow my excuse.

"True, true!" he said. "I understand. It is all very distressing . . . I wondered whether you were in agreement with the verdict."

"Oh, yes!" I said. "I can't see what other verdict they could have brought in."

We walked on for a minute or two in silence.

I was wondering, if the truth is to be told, just why the Professor had thought of coming over to see me this morning. He had

said that he had set out to call on me for the purpose of offering
his sympathy, and I suppose I ought not to have doubted his word.
But it seemed strange to me that such a busy man as he should be
willing to spare time from his university duties in order to visit me
personally when a short note would have served his purpose
equally well. I had seen him only about three times in my life, and
I had no reason to believe—though he was the kindest of men—
that he was moved by any particularly strong feelings for me. I say
nothing, I hope, that will give the impression that the Professor
was lacking in kindliness of heart—for he had that in an unusual
measure. What I would say is merely that my case did not seem to
merit so much solicitude.

"As I told you," he said at last, "the court seemed to be in some
doubt. They gave the 'misadventure' verdict, it would seem, because it was the—the most charitable verdict. You knew him very
well. You don't know of any circumstances in his life that might
make it possible to doubt the verdict?"

"No," I replied. "And really I did not know him so very well.
Until he appeared a few days ago I had not seen him for years—
two years at least."

"Oh!" he said. "I understood that you two were rather intimate
friends. Though it's not usual for cousins to be intimate friends,
when you come to think it over. You weren't enemies, I hope?"

"No," I assured him, hastily, whole-heartedly.

This cross-questioning, even from the Professor, was slightly
distasteful to me. I had a terrible secret—shared only by the faith-
ful Makepeace—to keep, and I must never allow anyone to suspect even that I had a secret, let alone to suspect that that secret
had anything to do with my cousin's death. Therefore I was eager
to assure him that there never had been the least bit of ill-feeling
between Mick and me.

"It's more usual," he said, with a vestige of a smile, "for cousins to be enemies than to be friends—especially in the case of two
brought up together, as I understand you two were. Brothers must
have a certain feeling of loyalty towards each other and towards
their own branch of the family. Friends are friends in spite of everything else. They are not influenced by family affairs. But cousins—the friendship of cousins is made difficult at every turn. They
can't ignore each other as friends who quarrel can, and the loyalty
of each to his own branch of the family makes for disputes rather
than for peace."

The Professor, with his rather tall figure and his white beard, looked and spoke very like a typical professor just then; and I sauntered along beside him wondering whether he were talking merely for the sake of talking or whether there were some design behind this call upon me and the remarks that had followed.

I assured him again that such relations as there had been between Mick and me had been of the very friendliest.

Soon after that he left me. We came to a point where the path was crossed by another, and here the Professor stopped.

"You'll excuse me if I leave you now," he said. "I am due to give a lecture in half an hour's time. Give my regards to Sylvia, won't you!"

He did not shake hands, but merely flourished his walking-stick in adieu and set off at a moderately brisk pace.

But he had not gone many steps when he stopped and came back. His hail arrested me as I, too, set off towards my destination.

"Have you heard," he said, when he had come quite close to me, "have you heard that the police are on the track of a man in connection with the murder of young Knight?"

I stared at him. He must have thought me slow of comprehension, but for a moment I was totally incapable of replying. Panic almost got the better of me. I felt myself to be in the midst of a web of circumstances wherein fact and fantasy, truth and misunderstanding were all so inextricably mixed that no one could say which was which—no one except Makepeace and me, and we dared not speak. The police were on the track of a man in connection with the murder of young Knight! They were on the track of an innocent man—for it was not a human being who had done that deed—and the innocent man might not be able to prove his innocence.

Would there be no end to the tragic effects of my unwitting invoking of that mysterious force!

"Oh?" I managed to say at length. "Do they think they'll catch him?"

"That I can't tell," he said. "But don't mention it to a soul. It has not been made public, only I happened to hear something, and I am telling you because you and he were such friends, and you, naturally, ought to know what is going on."

And before I could reply to that—before I could ask who the man was and for what reason the police suspected him—the Professor had bidden me a final good-bye and had gone.

Then it struck me that he had not remarked on the fact—so outstanding to me, and which I thought everyone must notice—that it was unusual for two separate violent deaths to occur among the friends of one man.

CHAPTER X

MR. ASHTON

THREE MONTHS PASSED. And three months is a long time in the life of a man in his early twenties. Even the unspeakable fears that had taken possession of me when it was proved beyond question that I was being watched over by a conscious, shadowy, and undoubtedly sinister presence could not maintain their intensity before the healing influence of three whole months. Time, youth, health, and the will not to dwell on morbid matters had brought me back almost to my usual light-heartedness.

And I had had much to do. The legal affairs in connection with the estate occupied me for a considerable time. And as I was now one of the wealthiest young bachelors in London I found that I had a great many more friends than I should ever have believed I had; and these friends seemed to make it their one business in life to see that I was never at a loss for some sort of entertainment. Even Professor Wetherhouse seemed to have become particularly attached to me, but that I put down to some natural liking on his part, for it was inconceivable that my fortune played any part in his having chosen me as one of his intimate friends.

Yet I was to have my suspicions about the Professor.

Only Sylvia remained the same. She was totally unaffected by my having inherited so much wealth. Perhaps she was thinking of the terrifying suspicions that had come to her when my cousin died, and was living on the borderland of fear. I could not tell, because I had kept discreetly silent on the subject when with her, knowing that time would cure her of the foolish superstitious belief that her lovers were destined to come to tragic ends.

I had given up my little place in Brompton Road and had, for the time being, taken a furnished flat in Grosvenor Square. Sylvia and I were to be married before the summer was out, and it was my intention to open up Bolton Towers again—which had remained closed for years, for Mick had had no interest in the place—and to take a Town house, and generally to live like a gentleman who knew what he was about.

I was discussing these matters with Sylvia one warm afternoon. We were alone by the open window of the drawing-room that looked out on to Park Lane lying beyond our precious patch of garden—for patches of garden *are* precious in Park Lane, costing I don't know how many pounds a square foot.

To me this was an occasion of almost inconceivable happiness. To be discussing plans for a future that embraced Sylvia and me as man and wife was to indulge in one of the highest delights of a thinking being—the delight of anticipation.

"And you and Lady Somerton will come down with me one day soon," I said, "and look over the place. And you will choose your own rooms. That will be a more difficult business than it sounds, for the place has been added to from time to time and it isn't easy to tell which are the principal rooms and which aren't. And the view from all sides is equally good, so that won't help you in your choice . . . And then there will be decorations to be thought of. You'll probably want to modernize some of the interiors . . . Oh, we'll have a splendid time!"

Sylvia smiled at that, but not so enthusiastically as I could have wished. I remember thinking, then, that perhaps I was putting a greater value on Bolton Towers than it merited. That, if it were so, was excusable, for I had lately realized how worrying would have been my position had I not inherited the estates and had I been compelled to try to make a show in life on about fifteen hundred a year. Or it might be that Sylvia, having been used to grandeur all her life, took grandeur as a matter of course, and could not work up a great deal of enthusiasm over even one of the stateliest of the stately homes of England.

"Do you think it will be necessary for us to go down beforehand?" she asked.

At that my face fell; but she added hurriedly, and with, I thought, a slight perturbation:

"I mean, wouldn't you rather that I left all that to you? It will be more delightful for me to go to the place for the first time after we are married. To go before will take all the novelty off the experience."

All of which I thought was rather excessive straining upon a weak excuse for not visiting Bolton Towers.

Her lack of enthusiasm had struck me, and now this unconvincing excuse struck me, and for the moment I wished that she were less beautiful, less mysteriously feminine, more easily affected, of commoner clay so that she might take more pleasure in the simple things of life. But when I looked at her as she turned her head for an instant to let her eyes roam over the golden pendants of a laburnum tree that grew close to the window, I knew that it was her distant, mysterious loveliness that had first attracted me and that I should always be content to worship without understanding or trying to understand.

I never thought to ask myself whether she loved me as much as I believed she did.

"And, in any case," she went on, turning from her contemplation of the laburnum tassels and fixing her gaze not on my eyes but on my necktie, "I should hate to disturb the decorations of such an old place. The charm of such a place as Bolton Towers lies in its being undisturbed from one generation to another. Don't you think so?"

I agreed on this comparatively minor point, though I might quite truthfully have said that I should be perfectly happy for her to take it into her head to have the entire place rebuilt.

I should have been almost glad if she were to exhibit some such piece of extravagant vanity, for I was disappointed in the calm manner in which she had accepted my suggestions.

Then I recollected that the only times on which she had shown any really glowing enthusiasm was when Christopher Knight entered the room on the evening of my introduction to her, and when she met Mick and me in the Park and took us back to lunch.

These two—Christopher and my cousin—seemed to have had the power to awaken what girlishness lay behind that mysterious reserve of hers. I had not been able to awaken it.

Yet I did not try to analyse that matter. I was too much of the worshipper to question her moods. It was sufficient for me that she was going to be my wife.

At that moment Lady Somerton came into the room, and looking about her and seeing us there she advanced towards us, her face lighting up into its usual animation.

Tea, she said, was waiting in the little drawing-room downstairs; and she took my arm as she spoke.

Sylvia preceded us out of the room and down the staircase; and at the half-landing I caught a glimpse of Lady Somerton's face. For that fraction of a second the animation had gone and she was looking at Sylvia, who was beginning to descend the second flight, with an expression half-questioning, half-annoyed. Almost at once she turned to me and continued her chatter about something or another—I forget what. But I had seen that glance of disapproval, and my loyalty towards my goddess sprang up within me.

I almost wished that Lady Somerton, who still had my arm, would openly remonstrate with Sylvia upon her lack of brightness—for that I took to be the reason for the disapproving glance at the bend of the staircase—so that I might have a chance of defending Sylvia and pointing out that there were qualities more desirable than effervescence of spirits.

Of course, no such chance presented itself, and I certainly could not have taken advantage of it if it had.

The Professor was in the little drawing-room, and he was talking confidentially with someone whom I had never seen before. They drew apart as we entered, and I had time to observe that the stranger was a middle-aged man of sturdy build whom I took to belong to one of the professions.

The stranger was introduced to me as Mr. Ashton, without any qualifying particulars. And over tea he continued to be referred to—when he was referred to, which was not often—as Mr. Ashton; and no hint was dropped regarding what particular Mr. Ashton he might be, or what his profession might be, or why he was present in the little drawing-room.

Mr. Ashton himself spoke little. I doubt whether he said three words during all the time that we spent over tea. This fact was very noticeable because at Lady Somerton's the people one met were invariably well-known people, and a newcomer was encouraged to talk. Most of them, I might say, did not require encouragement.

It was after tea that the Professor took me aside.

"You were telling me the other day," said the Professor, "that you would soon have to be on the look-out for a male secretary. Now that money has made your life so much more complicated, as you were saying, I suppose a secretary is a necessity. To most of us such a person is a luxury. But that's beside the point. I want to ask you whether you would care to take Ashton for the job. He is a man I used to know very well. But I understand that life has not been too good to him, and I thought—"

So that was the reason for the appearance of the uncommunicative Mr. Ashton! It was rather an unusual method, I thought, of introducing a prospective employee to a prospective employer; but it had this peculiar feature about it, namely, that I could not possibly refuse to accept Mr. Ashton there and then to fill the post.

I did accept him. I accepted him without asking for any particulars regarding his abilities, without asking for any particulars whatsoever. The fact that the Professor had recommended him answered everything favourably before it was asked.

Later I had a quiet, formal talk with Mr. Ashton himself.

I had expected him to be a cultured man, of course; and in that I was not disappointed. But I remember thinking it queer that life had not been too good to him—an expression of the Professor's signifying, in the circumstances, that Ashton couldn't find work. It seemed queer because of the fact that Ashton's manner was that of a man who has a calm and easy confidence in himself, and who has not had his spirit cowed by a series of defeats. His personality was forceful, albeit he said little. And though he called me sir after almost every phrase, I had the feeling that he was my superior in every way and, moreover, that he was perfectly well aware of the fact.

In short, he made me feel something of an upstart, and made me almost ashamed of the accident of birth that had put me in the rôle of master and him in the rôle of servant.

Had I been free to choose I should have chosen a younger man for my secretary—one to whom I could state a command without having the feeling that I was begging a favour. But the Professor had caught me on the hop—not, did I think, intentionally—and I could do nothing but take Mr. Ashton into my service, hoping, no doubt, to acquire a commanding dignity in time.

And, all that being settled, the Professor and Mr. Ashton left together.

They had barely been gone five minutes, and Lady Somerton was only just beginning to interest me with an account of a social function that she had attended on the previous day, when a maid came in to announce Mr. Wetherhouse.

This was Sydney, the Professor's son, and this was the first time I had seen him for months.

He had not changed. He stood for an instant in the doorway, with his mild, courtly smile, and then stepped up to Lady Somerton; and after a formal greeting and a bow to Sylvia and me, he explained that he was looking for his father.

"He has just gone," said Lady Somerton. "Not five minutes ago. Perhaps you can catch him up."

I thought it rather curious that Lady Somerton should say such a thing, because a moment's reflection would have told her that five minutes was long enough to take the Professor half a mile off in any direction; and as the Professor had a strong liking for taxis and would likely be whizzing along in one at the moment, Lady Somerton's suggestion had nothing to recommend it.

"Oh, that is all right!" said young Wetherhouse. "He will have gone on to his club. I'll follow him there. It isn't an important matter."

It seemed to me that Lady Somerton had become less animated since young Wetherhouse's entry. With me she was invariably pleasant. She was one of those women in the forties who have retained a slim figure and a fascinating liveliness. She was dark, of course. Fair women in the forties usually show signs of plumpness. Life sat lightly upon her ladyship, and no doubt that accounted for her charm and for her almost invariable happiness; and it was that that made me observe that she showed less of her usual manner towards young Sydney Wetherhouse.

The tea-things were still in evidence, and she asked the young man whether he had had tea. He answered that he had, though I had a suspicion that he was not telling the truth.

The four of us chatted together about nothing in particular for another ten minutes or so, and then young Wetherhouse took his leave.

But during those ten minutes I learned, by simple observation, that the admiration for Sylvia, with which I had credited this young man when last I saw him, was still alive. One could not mistake the meaning of the way in which his eyes were attracted to her during pauses in the conversation; and though at heart I was sorry, I was sufficiently human to be elated at the thought that other men admired the woman who was going to be my wife.

And I wondered whether Lady Somerton, too, had noticed that young Wetherhouse was still in love with Sylvia. I think she did. I think so not only because any observant person would be almost sure to notice it, but because of the change in her manner when he arrived.

It seemed that she was keeping him at arm's length. Though as Sylvia was soon to marry me and as young Wetherhouse had made no move all these months to put himself into the running for Sylvia's hand, I thought Lady Somerton's attitude rather extreme.

I was to learn later that her ladyship was not given to taking up extreme attitudes in any matter without sufficient reason.

In the meantime, the three of us were left alone chatting over the remains of the tea. At least, Lady Somerton and I were chatting. Sylvia, when Sydney Wetherhouse left the room, had not re-

sumed a chair, but had gone wandering about, examining orna-
ments and appearing to be listening to our chatter.

I happened to look up. Sylvia had wandered towards one of the
windows which overlooked that precious patch of garden wherein
the delicate laburnum bloomed.

She was standing with the curtain in one hand, and her attitude
of pensiveness struck me as symbolic of the mystery that had always clung about her—the mystery of her distant, maddening
femininity which I could never understand, and which, in fact, had
been growing more distant and more maddening of late.

Then I saw her give a sudden movement and half raise her free
hand.

I got up, as casually as I could, and strolled over towards her,
talking to Lady Somerton the while. She turned at my approach
and would have herded me back to where her aunt sat; but I was
not to be turned aside in that manner.

I took her arm in mine, with a smile, advancing far enough to
see the black and white mosaic path that led down to the pavement.

And on the pavement, turning away from the gate, was young
Wetherhouse.

"Speeding the parting guest!" I remarked, not with any ulterior
meaning; for how could I imagine then that Sylvia, who was going
to marry me in a few weeks' time, should be carrying on even a
mild intrigue with that shy boy?

If she were disconcerted by my having seen her making a gesture towards young Wetherhouse I did not notice it, and we returned towards the centre of the room.

"I have had a secretary forced upon me," I told them, as we
stood together in a group just before my departure.

"Forced upon you?" laughed Lady Somerton.

"Literally forced upon me," I protested. "In the matter of a private secretary one should have a perfectly free choice. And one
should be as careful in choosing one's secretary as in choosing
one's wife. But—"

"You can always dismiss a secretary," remarked Sylvia.

"Almost as easily as you can dismiss a wife these days," put in
Lady Somerton. "But go on. You were saying—?"

"I was saying that the Professor has deprived me of my rights
by forcing me to accept Mr. Ashton. Or by introducing Mr. Ashton
to me, which amounts to the same thing."

"Mr. Ashton!" exclaimed both the ladies at once.

"I wondered why the Professor brought Mr. Ashton along here this afternoon," added Lady Somerton.

"And *I* was wondering all the time," said Sylvia, "where I had met Mr. Ashton before. I am still wondering. I'm sure I have met him, but I'm equally sure that I don't know anybody of the name of Ashton."

The mildly puzzling position had brought a look of animation to Sylvia's face such as it had lacked during the greater part of the afternoon.

"Now that you mention it, Sylvia," said her ladyship, with a frown, "I thought that there was something familiar about the man . . . Ashton? Ashton?"

But neither the frown nor the repetition of the name brought forth anything definite regarding my new secretary; and I took my leave almost at once, promising to let them know how Mr. Ashton behaved himself.

CHAPTER XI

THE THING

DURING ALL THIS TIME the fears to which I had once been a prey had been gradually sinking into slumber, and I could think of the two deaths without any sense of horror. Even the story told by Makepeace—who, since our removal to Grosvenor Square, had wonderfully recovered his pride and well-being— even that story now seemed rather fantastic. I had learnt that it is not possible to experience any emotion intensively, by recollection at least, for any length of time, whether it be an emotion of pleasure or an emotion of pain.

The whole ghastly business had faded into the past—not only in my mind but in the minds of everybody else. The police had apparently given up the search for the murderer of Christopher Knight. Nothing more had been heard of the suspect whom the Professor had mentioned some months ago.

But that there were queer things still going on around me I was soon to learn.

Mr. Ashton had now taken up his duties as my secretary. Of course, he lived in the flat. In one way and another quite a lot of people lived in the flat. I had given Makepeace a free hand in the arranging of the domestic side of my existence, and he had exercised this free hand in a really royal manner. It seemed to me, after my long period of careful living, that one young man could not possibly want so many attendants to look after his personal comfort; but Makepeace was of a different opinion. And I had not the courage to disagree with him. I could not forget the care with which, in the Brompton Road days, he used to save fractions of coppers off my electric light bill, and I could not now deny him the glory of an imposing domestic staff. For the glory was his, not mine. I had absorbed some of the detached grandeur of spirit that Sylvia showed in these matters, and I could not work up great enthusiasm over having three times as many servants as I required.

Mr. Ashton, alone of the household that must have numbered eight or ten people all told, dined with me. Although I had not yet mustered up sufficient dignity to give him a single command, the work that he was paid to do did not suffer. I had been uneasy about my ability to instruct him as a master should instruct a servant, but when it came down to practice I found that there was no need to instruct him. He was the perfect secretary—so far as I, who had never had a secretary, could tell—and the frightening pile of unanswered letters that had stood beneath an unsteadily poised paperweight on my desk vanished within the first few days. Where they vanished to I did not inquire; but as most of them seemed to be signed by other secretaries-secretaries of this, that and the other league for this, that and the other purpose—I supposed that Mr. Ashton had dealt with them in his own way and according to his own opinion of their merits, for he never once asked me to sign a cheque.

One night I came home unusually late. I had been to a theatre with some of my club friends, and after the theatre we had gone on to the club. For some time I had been suffering from sleeplessness, and I had got into the habit of keeping late hours in the belief—mistaken, I think—that by tiring myself out I should sleep better.

And to tire myself out further on this particular night I had walked from the eastern end of Pall Mall, so that it was getting on for two o'clock in the morning when I found myself in Grosvenor Square.

But late as I was, I reflected, as I walked up the steps of the block in which I had my flat and in which Makepeace had his retinue of servants, there was someone even later than I; for as I looked about the square, which at that time lay solemn and ghostly, I saw a man enter it by the same way as I had come.

I took no particular notice of him, only remarking that he was in a dark grey suit so far as the distance and the uncertain lamplight permitted me to judge.

When I looked for him again, as I stepped through the main doorway of the building, he had disappeared.

I remember the incident, because the incident of a brother wayfarer in Grosvenor Square at two o'clock in the morning is likely to be remembered. I remember it also because it was associated, however accidentally, with the first of a new series of mysterious happenings.

I had told Makepeace never to wait up for me after eleven o'clock. He had demurred at first, for he was a bit of a tyrant towards me and would not allow me to deprive him of the smallest part of his duties without making a fight for it. But I had made him obey me in this, and had told him that if I were later than eleven I should have to bear the discomfort of disposing of my own hat and coat and finding my way to bed unattended. The subtlety of that was lost upon Makepeace; but I gained my point.

On this particular night—or morning—I opened the flat door noiselessly and stepped quickly into the darkened hall.

As I did so, I thought I heard a sound near at hand—just the breath of movement with nothing to distinguish its source. I was conscious, too, of a presence. I could see nothing, for there was only blackness about me. And, after the first sound, I could hear nothing. But there was in the air that indefinable something that tells us we are not alone.

It was but a couple of seconds before I had reached the switch and flooded the place with light.

There, against the farther wall, stood Makepeace, his eyes blinking because of the sudden brightness, and his face grey. Whether this last was an illusion caused by the quick transition from darkness to brilliance I could not tell. And I could not tell, moreover, whether the sudden light was responsible for his shrinking attitude.

"Hallo!" I said, quickly recovering myself. "What's the matter? What are you standing there for?"

It was the dark hall and the manner of his standing in the dark hall that struck me; otherwise, I should merely have said, "Why aren't you in bed?"

He came forward then. The greyness of his face was still evident, and I concluded that it was not due to the light.

"I—I thought I heard something, sir," he said.

"Where?" I asked. I think my tone conveyed impatience, but at that moment I was not sure whether I trusted Makepeace's words or not. It was seldom that he was other than deliberate in his utterance, and in this case there was a hesitation that did not escape me.

"In your bedroom, sir."

"What did you hear?"

Again Makepeace hesitated.

"I can't rightly say, sir. It might have been a chair being moved, or it might have been the door into the study shutting."

"Have you looked?" 1 asked him, stepping towards my bedroom door as I spoke.

"No," he said. "I was waiting here. I wasn't sure whether you had come in or not."

I stood with the bedroom door-knob in my hand, listening. Then I threw the door wide quickly and switched on the light.

The bedroom lay silent and innocent.

I stepped within and listened at the door that communicated with my study; and I threw that open in the same way, letting the light from the bedroom shine into the small chamber. The study, too, was empty and had the same look of innocence.

"You must have been dreaming," I said.

"No," he began in a very certain voice. Then he half turned on his heel, and said, "Well, perhaps I was dreaming."

"Or perhaps it was one of your servants," I suggested. I always referred to them as his servants, but he was slow to appreciate my kind of humour.

"No," he said. "They are all at the other side of that door"— meaning a green-baize door at the back of the hall—"and none of them dare come in here without my permission. Nobody is this side of that door after nine o'clock at night except you, sir, and me, and Mr. Ashton."

"And Mr. Ashton is in bed?"

"Yes, sir."

Mr. Ashton had the honour of having a bedroom on this side of "that" door.

"Then you've been dreaming, Makepeace," I concluded. "You had better go back to bed. The night air, even in summer, won't do you much good."

He was turning away, and had reached the hall, when I recalled him.

"How is it that you are fully dressed?" I asked; for he was dressed correctly in every detail exactly as I had seen him when I left the flat immediately after dinner. "Haven't you been to bed?"

He came back into the room.

"No, sir. I—I didn't feel like sleep, sir."

"But that's preposterous!" I exclaimed. "You're up before seven in the mornings, and you're on the go all day. You must be dead tired by eleven at night. Didn't feel like sleep? I don't believe you."

Saying that, I stepped behind him and shut the door.

"Now tell me what this means!" I demanded.

My attitude took him by surprise. I was glad I had suddenly adopted such an attitude. Had I been wrong in my assumption that there was something in my old servant's behaviour that required explanation, I should have felt unspeakably sorry for having doubted his assertion that he could not sleep, for my doubt would have pained him excessively. But I could see at once that I had not been wrong.

"What is it?" I asked. "You might as well tell me. You can't expect me to believe that you have been waiting up, fully dressed, in case you might happen to hear a noise."

"Well, Mister Martin," he said, adopting, instinctively, the name by which he had known me for so many years, so that I knew something significant was to follow, "that's just what I was waiting up for—in case I might happen to hear a noise. You say I can't expect you to believe it. But I hope you will believe it, Mister Martin."

I looked at him with a different interest.

"But I don't understand," I said. "What made you think that you might hear a noise? Explain it all, Makepeace; I don't follow you at all."

And though I was right in saying that I did not follow him, I was almost certain that his behaviour had to do with the secret that was shared between him and me—the dreadful family secret that he had disclosed to me some months ago.

We had never mentioned it since that time. There had been no need to mention it. I, for my part, had been only too glad to let it sink out of sight, and not to disturb its slow sinking. Makepeace must have been of the same mind, hoping, no doubt, that it would lie dormant for another decade.

"I told you a lie, Mister Martin," he said. "I didn't hear anything to-night. But I heard something last night."

"Where? In this room?" I asked. "What did you hear?"

Makepeace, I could see, was in genuine trouble. He did not want to speak. But that made me only the more determined to know what was in his mind.

"I insist on your telling me, Makepeace," I said. "I insist on it, so you might as well tell me now as later."

"Well, then I will," he said, as though to state that the responsibility was no longer his. "And it wasn't only what I heard, Mister Martin, though that was queer enough: it was what I saw . . . Did you sleep well last night, sir?"

"Yes," I told him. "Strangely enough I did. I haven't been sleeping very well lately. What then?"

"Well, I waited for you to come in. I went to bed, I might say, but I knew I shouldn't sleep until you were in. Then I heard the flat door open and I heard you go to your room, and I could hear you moving about for a good while after that, and then everything grew quiet. But I couldn't sleep.

"And then I heard somebody talking. I thought it was you, Mister Martin. But when I listened I could hear that it wasn't you, and that it wasn't talking. It was singing. Leastways, it was something between the two. And it was coming from this room. To make sure I got up and opened my door a bit wider; and it *was* coming from this room—the eeriest, mournfulest sound you ever hear, and that's a fact, sir. In the dead of night, too. It did give me a turn, that it did. I thought of what you and I had spoken about that night after Mister Michael died—you know what I mean, Mister Martin—and I thought that this was it. And I stood there listening, and trying to make up my mind what to do. But I didn't seem to be able to move, for the thing went on and on without a stop. And the place was all that quiet and that dark, and nothing but this weird sing-song going on, that it made my hair fairly stand on end. I might have stood there all night, getting more scared every minute, but I thought that maybe it was you after all, and that you were ill perhaps. So I put out my hand and switched the light on, and went to your door and called you. The noise stopped at once, and I thought I heard somebody moving. And as you didn't answer I thought that was queerer than ever, for you would have said you were all right if you were all right. I fair lost my head then, for you can guess what I was thinking, and I opened the door right wide. And I saw something—but I can't for the life of me say what it was. It was something disappearing into the study there. It might have been a man. It might have been—something else. I don't know. It just disappeared—flick!—as I opened the door, and the room being half dark—"

"Why didn't you wake me?" I asked, my eyes fixed on the old man's grey face as they had been throughout the whole of his narrative, my voice sounding harsh and strange in my own ears.

I felt that the blood had left my face. A physical uneasiness had gripped me as though there might be some sinister being glaring at me from behind. I pictured myself lying asleep on the bed there (with heaven knew what weirdness going on around me) all unconscious of danger.

"I did try to wake you, sir," Makepeace answered. "But I couldn't. At first I thought—well, I didn't know what I would find. But you were all right. I touched you and I shook you, and then you said something in your sleep so I knew you were all right. But I couldn't wake you."

"Queer, that," I said, "for I've been sleeping badly of late. Did you go—"

"Did I go into the study?" Makepeace asked, anticipating my question. "I did not, sir. Not for anything in this world or the next would I have—"

"Of course not," I said.

It was thoughtless of me to have suggested such a thing.

"With that moaning and chanting," Makepeace went on, "and the flick of that thing when I opened the door, and you, sir, lying there neither dead nor alive nor awake nor yet asleep, as you might say—"

"I understand."

"It would have taken a less scared man than me to go into that room."

I glanced towards the study as he spoke. The small room was sinister in its stillness. The light entering it by the communicating door struck my desk, which was in the middle of the carpet, and made it stand out distinctly; but the rest was in half darkness or deep shadow—the bookcases, the door leading through into the hall, the polished floor beyond the edge of the carpet—deep shadow and mystery.

"And what happened then? What was the voice saying? Could you make out?"

"No, that I couldn't. It was saying something, but it was such a sing-song sort of way of speaking that I couldn't catch any sense in it at all . . . Then I put on the light at the top of your bed, and sat down beside you, facing the study door there. That was all I could do. And the light was that eerie! It was just shining on the bed and on you. But do you think I could get up and cross to the door to put the big light on! Not for a fortune! And as for creeping over and shutting the study door—! So I just sat there—watching for something to happen. But nothing happened, and you slept on, and it got light again. But I've had the creeps all day."

The grey, aged face of Makepeace invested the moment with a peculiar horror. It seemed that he and I were alone and at the mercy of this mystery that had clung about my family for generations. My recent attempts at dismissing the terror by sheer force of will now appeared pitiful. Even to succeed in forgetting it for a time was nothing. And though there should be no further manifestation during my whole life, there would always be expectant terror, for now I and not others had become the object of the manifestations.

"Makepeace," I said, taking his hand. "You are the best friend I ever had."

My fears had made me overlook the night of terror that the old man had spent for my sake, sitting there hour after hour, his eyes never leaving the dark doorway of the sinister study.

"If it hadn't been for you," I went on, "I might not be alive now." And I thought, for a fleeting second, though I did not say it: "And that might have been a good thing."

"And you never told me," I went on. "Why didn't you?"

"I don't know, Mister Martin," he said." I didn't know what to do. I didn't want to tell you. Leastways I thought I might wait a day or two and see if anything else happened."

"And you were going to watch at nights?"

"Yes. You see, nothing else might happen, I thought; and maybe there would be no call to scare you. But however—"

There was a pause.

"If I may make the suggestion," said Makepeace, hesitatingly, "I think it would be as well for me to sleep in this room. We could have a bed brought in to-morrow. That is—"

I agreed readily. That had been in my mind, but I had been afraid to suggest it. Yet something would have had to be done. I should have been afraid to shut my eyes at nights, and that would have been an impossible existence.

"What about Mr. Ashton?" I asked. "It will be too much for you. The nervous strain night after night, I mean. It will be bad enough for me, but I'm young."

I spoke as though I were not in the most abject terror at the thought of night following night and my never knowing when the fatal night would arrive.

"We must keep this to ourselves, Mister Martin," he said. "If rumours began to get about, there is no saying what folks might think. There are two deaths that have not been rightly explained away. You never know."

"Yes," I agreed. "We must keep it to ourselves."

The law, I realized, did not consider the existence of ghosts. People who maintained that ghosts committed murders might be suspected by the law.

CHAPTER XII

EAVESDROPPING

THE DAWN was beginning to break when Makepeace and I, with a great deal left unsaid, parted—I to my bath, he to the kitchen to prepare some tea.

The greyness of the early morning was almost as eerie as the blackness of night; and though, for some reason having its basis in superstition, I was not now afraid of attack. I was acutely conscious of a creeping physical uneasiness that made me start at shadows and that made me want to be continually looking behind me.

And there was no rule by which I could gauge either the motive behind these supernatural phenomena or the extent of them. Until this latest manifestation there had been one constant feature that had provided a more or less scientific basis upon which to reason: the outrages had all been committed following upon a feeling of extreme jealousy on the part of some one of my family, and the victim had been the one who was the object of that jealousy.

But now the power—whatever it might be—was apparently exerting itself against me, whereas it had formerly exerted itself in my behalf. And there was no Strange left who could call the power into activity—assuming that the power was dependent for impulse upon the wish of a Strange.

The constant feature had been disturbed. There was no means of judging what might happen next—unless, as occurred to me suddenly as I was stepping under the cold shower, the spirit was now intent upon destroying me, the last of the family.

But no reasoning could be conclusive. I had not now any knowledge by which to reassure myself. I could only wait for the next drawing aside of the curtain behind which lurked the mystery.

I rejoined Makepeace in the bedroom where he had now arrived with the morning cup of tea. There were two cups of tea on the tray and two plates containing biscuits. Even Makepeace's strict—I thought false—sense of position had been broken down by his ordeal of two nights ago.

Over this tea we arranged that he should move into my room sometime during that day. No one need or would know of the alteration in this part of the establishment, for Makepeace was very jealous of his position and would on no account allow any of the other servants to attend to me personally.

We did not discuss the tremendous mystery that lay at the back of this alteration in the domestic arrangements. It would not bear discussion.

That day I went to Park Lane for lunch. And, despite the curse that was hanging over my house and that might destroy me at any moment, I went with as great an enthusiasm as I should have felt had I been the most normal of beings and had my expectations of a rapturous existence with Sylvia been brilliantly unclouded. The bright sunshine and the crowds in the Park might have had something to do with my being thus easily able to shake off the fears of the night. But I think that Sylvia had more to do with it. At all costs I must not allow Sylvia to know what was hanging over me. And, in any case, why should I carry my fears into the daytime? They belonged to the night. In the daytime they existed only by recollection. I thought, as I walked down Park Lane, and the buses whizzed towards me on the left and the Park railings rose beside me on the right, and hundreds and hundreds of people within my view went about their business or their pleasure: "I'm not afraid now. I don't feel that there is a sinister presence creeping up stealthily behind me. And if there is, it doesn't matter. It can't harm me physically, because of all these people. And it can't harm me through fear—as I'm told is the way with things supernatural—simply because in daylight and in company I don't feel fear."

And these thoughts, as I walked down Park Lane between the speedy traffic on the one hand and the holiday atmosphere of the sunlit Park on the other, brought such a brightness of spirits as to make me think that I had positively and miraculously conquered the terrors of the other world. I knew, of course, by experience, that night would find me a different being; but my chance of happiness lay in not thinking of the night.

I was early for the luncheon appointment. As a matter of fact, I had not troubled to notice the exact time. Luncheon was at one o'clock; but I was now such a frequent visitor to the house that I might wander in an hour before the appointed time without causing anybody to raise questioning eyebrows. Even the servants—even the suspicious fellow whom I frequently found posted in the hall—honoured me by not submitting my visits to the usual elaborate rites by which the sanctity of the home is protected, and I was free to walk in or out as though the place were my own.

I crossed Park Lane and walked up the black and white mosaic path and mounted the steps to the front door. The front door stood open to the warm air. I walked into the deserted hall, paused a while to enjoy its coolness, put my hat and gloves on the oak rug-chest, and strolled casually through into the dim interior, guided by the sound of voices which I guessed came from that little room at the back—the little panelled room where I had declared my love to Sylvia.

I was sorry to hear these voices. The clock in the hall told me that I had half an hour to spare, and I should have welcomed half an hour alone with Sylvia. I was rarely alone with her for more than a few minutes at a time. We had not had a heart to heart talk for weeks. I tried to recall the last time we had had a heart to heart talk, and I could not.

And that thought, as I stood at the back of the hall uncertain what to do, brought me to the realization that I had never indulged in scenes of intense tenderness with Sylvia. There had been moments of strong emotion, such as that in the Park on the morning after Christopher Knight's death and such as that on the evening after my cousin's death, but these had had their origin in the dramatic intensity of circumstances and were not brought about by Sylvia's tenderness for me.

And now I felt that my love-making had lacked just that exchange of tendernesses. Our courtship had been born of dramatic intensity. I had happened to be at hand when circumstances had overwhelmed Sylvia, when she had been most susceptible to the influence of a new acquaintance; and I had taken advantage of the circumstances. Sylvia had accepted my love, and I had been content with her mere acceptance. The honour of possessing so much beauty had contented me. Yet I had missed that foolish, delightful "spooning" that seems to characterize the period of courtship.

"It might be," I said to myself as I took a step nearer to the door of the little panelled room—"it might be that she is still worried by the coincidence of the two deaths. It must have seemed queer to her, and she had some justification for the thought that she was at the bottom of them. Women are very superstitious, I believe."

We had never mentioned that matter after her hysterical outburst on the night when we learned of Mick's death. But perhaps it was still present in her mind—or perhaps she had given all her love to young Christopher and could not repeat the emotion in its full intensity. Lately I had been noticing her quietness, and these questions had been occupying my mind.

The door of the little panelled room was half open. I listened for the sound of Sylvia's voice, intending, if I did not hear it, to roam into some of the other public rooms in search of her.

The murmur of conversation was indistinct, and I had to go within a few paces of the door in order to hear who was speaking.

The Professor was one. I was now in the corridor almost opposite the half-open door, and the voices suddenly became clear.

"Very well," said the Professor. "I doubted very much whether I should succeed in convincing you. And as you will not be convinced," (I pictured him shrugging his shoulders) "you must take the consequences."

"But," replied the voice of Lady Somerton, with a touch of hauteur, "you have not attempted to convince me of anything. If you were to tell me what was in your mind you might succeed in convincing me. But simply to ask me to trust you—and on a point that means so much to Sylvia, and to me—"

Lady Somerton did not finish the sentence. It had more meaning when left unfinished. I saw her, in my imagination, turning from the Professor in that characteristic way of hers, in order to let her words sink home.

And I—who regarded eavesdropping with abhorrence—stood listening. Yes, I held my breath and was not ashamed. The mention of Sylvia's name and the unmistakable tone of antagonism between these two made me stand where I was. If the matter they were discussing was of so much importance to Sylvia—who, I guessed, was not present—then very likely it had to do with me. Perhaps not. But most likely it had, for the supreme fact of Sylvia's existence at the moment was her approaching marriage to me. In any case, I listened.

"But I have explained," went on the Professor, "that I dare not say outright what I think. The whole thing is of such a very delicate nature that I am afraid to reduce my fears to plain words. Our information at this early stage is too imperfect, and our knowledge of the subject is too vague, to allow us to state our suspicions definitely. All I ask is—"

"Sydney is in love with her," put in Lady Somerton, ignoring his attempt at explaining his reasons for withholding information.

I instinctively drew back half a step, praying that no one might come along the corridor and so disturb my eavesdropping.

"Please," he said, in a hurt tone, "please credit me with disinterested motives, at least! I do agree that Sydney is very fond of her, and some months ago I thought that she was not wholly averse to Sydney. But please leave Sydney's name out of it. His affairs have nothing directly to do with my speaking to you now. His disappointment is nothing compared with what is in my mind."

"Well, what *is* in your mind?" she persisted. "If you would only give me a hint about what you are driving at—"

"Oh, dear! Oh, dear!" exclaimed the Professor, and I could hear the sound of steps and knew that he was pacing the floor, impatient because of Lady Somerton's inability or unwillingness to understand him.

As for me, I was for the time incapable of motion. Had the door opened fully and had they suddenly come forth from the room, they would have caught me unmistakably in the act of listening. I could not have gathered my wits together sufficiently well even to make a pretence of being about to knock at the door; for my mind had jumped to the conclusion that the Professor had hit upon my secret. Naturally I would jump to that conclusion. My secret—shared only by Makepeace—was my most carefully guarded possession. If it were known that the supernatural had designs upon me—that, in the popular phrase, I was haunted—there would be an end of all my joy in life. I should be shunned. I should be someone apart, with whom the normal and happily innocent of mankind could have no social dealings. Perhaps circumstances would enable me to lay the ghost, and then I could live happily; but until then I must guard my secret by every means within my power.

Little wonder, hearing the Professor, that I feared the worst!

"I need not mention," said Lady Somerton, "that I have a fair amount of tact and discretion—even though I am a woman." There was a ring of cruel irony in her voice. "Anything that you might tell me will not be repeated. That goes without saying."

Yet she said it. I was sorry for the Professor then. Lady Somerton was persistent almost to the point of rudeness.

"I know, I know!" he said. "But please accept my word. I dare not tell you—simply dare not. As I say, the field of inquiry has not yet been thoroughly investigated, and I have not the knowledge necessary to enable me to prove my case. I can only suspect; but even the little knowledge we have makes me sure that my suspicions are correct. And until I can prove that my suspicions are correct—a very different thing!—I dare not state them. I dare not state them even to you, Lady Somerton."

There was a moment or two of silence. I could picture the two of them in there, the conclave having reached a deadlock, standing pondering, each trying to think of the next word.

"Not even to you," the Professor said again, as though to break the silence. "It is too horrible."

"Horrible?"

"If it is true, yes. And I think it is true. All that I ask is that you put the wedding off for a time—a month, say. Much might happen in a month."

There was another silence.

"You make me afraid," said Lady Somerton at length. "I don't know what you mean, and that makes it so much worse. The first thing that springs to one's mind when you speak about a field of inquiry that has not been thoroughly investigated is the spirit world. But it can't have anything to do with that. Has it?"

But the Professor would not fall into the trap.

"I must refuse to say anything whatever about what it might be. I merely ask you to use your influence in trying to have the wedding postponed. You will do that?"

"Oh, I don't see how I can!"

"Very well. If you don't, I will. But don't be afraid: I shan't mention it to Sylvia—not until I can state definitely that my suspicions are correct. It would be an unpardonable unkindness to mention it before. There is just a possibility that I may be wrong; and, in any event, there is no reflection, as I have told you, upon the young man."

"I hope you may be wrong in whatever you suspect. I pray you may be wrong." Lady Somerton's voice had suddenly become very quiet.

"I also pray that I may be wrong."

"And you'll forgive me," said Lady Somerton, "for suggesting that you were speaking on behalf of Sydney. I ought not to have said that. I didn't really mean it. I had to try to account for your strange request in some way."

"Quite! Quite!" exclaimed the Professor, in a noticeably kind voice. "You are eager for the marriage to take place, aren't you?"

"I am very happy about it," she replied. "I took to Martin the first time I saw him. But I hear that people are saying it is his wealth that is making the marriage."

"Oh, I'm sure it isn't," the Professor assured her hurriedly. "And I don't think people are saying that."

But he spoke so earnestly that I, listening, was certain that he did not believe what he said. People were saying that my wealth was making the marriage? That was interesting, but it had little enough significance to me at that moment. I failed to see then what I saw later, namely, that there must be some reason for what people were saying, and that perhaps Sylvia's lack of enthusiasm and Lady Somerton's eagerness for the marriage were a true indication of the state of affairs.

But, as I say, these things had little enough significance at the moment. In fact, I hardly took any notice of the latter part of the conversation. My mind was concerned, fearfully, intensely, with the Professor's disclosures. How he had got on the track of my secret I could not fathom; but that he had got on the track of it was obvious in every word that he had spoken.

Of course it was a thing that he dared not hint at! And of course it was horrible! And of course there was no reflection on my character!

I slipped along the corridor to the hall again. I had heard all that I wanted to hear.

I was alarmed, but not unduly alarmed. In fact, I took it with marvellous calm. I knew that the Professor dared not speak until he had conclusively laid bare my secret, and in doing that (though how he could hope to do it, I did not know) he might succeed in solving the mystery and thus freeing me from my terrible fears.

I picked up my hat and gloves from the rug-chest, and when Lady Somerton and the Professor sauntered through into the hall a few minutes later they found me standing in a negligent attitude surveying the section of Park Lane that was framed by the oblong of the doorway.

"Ah, Martin!" exclaimed the Professor. "Here you are!"

The Professor did not usually address me, "Ah, Martin!" He invariably called me by my surname, thus raising me to the status of mature manhood. The "Ah, Martin!" suggested the father addressing the fledgling.

Lady Somerton shook hands. In her handshake and in the few words of welcome that she muttered there was a trace of nervousness, which I pretended not to notice.

The Professor, too, shook hands—not a frequent habit of his; and I detected—for I was keyed up to observe subtleties of expression and manner—an immense kindliness in his glance. He was not afraid to meet my eyes, as Lady Somerton was. He suspected my secret, and he was moved by pity for me.

I ought to have appreciated that. But did I?

I did not. In my soul I said: "Confound you and your pity and your kindliness and your fatherliness and your fields of inquiry that have not been thoroughly investigated!"

That was unreasonable, I know. But it was in accordance with the psychology governing the individual who finds himself set apart from the herd.

"And you think you're going to postpone the wedding!" the perverse demon within me went on, as I watched the Professor descend the steps. "You think you're going to postpone the wedding until you can prove or disprove your theories about the spirit world! Well, you just aren't!"

CHAPTER XIII

SUNLIT HORROR

THAT AFTERNOON I had a surprise visit from the Professor.
I had not had my desired *tête-à-tête* with Sylvia. She had appeared in the hall not half a minute before lunch was due to begin, and she and Lady Somerton and I had gone into the dining-room together.

The sight of her, as she quietly joined us when we turned back from seeing the Professor off, doubly confirmed me in my determination that the wedding arrangements should not be interfered with. She displayed no excessive joy at seeing me. Her face did not light up. She welcomed me in level tones. She gave up not one shred of that feminine mystery in which she was enveloped.

But that fostered my pride wonderfully. Had she been freer in her manner she would have been less sublime, and I would have been less maddened by her beauty. The fact that over-ruled everything else in her relations with me was the fact that she and I were about to be married. In the light of that, smiles and kisses and fondlings were as naught.

I left immediately after lunch, and returned to Grosvenor Square.

I had a great deal to think about, but I deliberately tried not to think about anything in particular. Yet I could not for long keep my mind off what I had overheard. That my secret was in danger of being discovered was a source of very real fear and uneasiness. The other—the dread of another visitation such as that which had occurred two nights ago—was much more intense while it lasted. It was an ordeal that no strength of will could overcome, and its contemplation, in the setting of the dark, silent flat, was enough to bring dampness to one's forehead, as it had brought dampness to my forehead while I listened to Makepeace's recital of the visitation. But in the daytime its power was negligible.

The discovery of my secret, however, was another matter. It was a practical matter. It was a fear less horrible—not horrible at all compared with the brooding terror of night. But it was always with me—at night and in the daytime—and it might rob me of Sylvia and leave me alive to know of my loss. The mysterious force that was haunting me might also rob me of Sylvia, but it would do so only by killing me—or Sylvia—as it had killed Christopher Knight and my cousin. But the Professor could bring about that which would be worse than death—namely, life without Sylvia. I was so completely enthralled by her ineffable beauty that I could not contemplate life without her.

The thought struck me that I might enlist the sympathies of the Professor. With my assistance he might succeed in ridding me of the terror that might otherwise make my nights fearsome throughout the rest of my existence. And if he could do that he would then offer no resistance to my marriage with Sylvia.

But I dismissed the thought. The risk was too great. The odds against his solving the mystery were many chances to one. I could not afford to stake my secret on such an improbable hope. My desire for Sylvia was greater than my dread of the unknown.

The spacious grandeur of Grosvenor Square lay peacefully under the sweltering early afternoon sunshine. The gardens in the middle of the Square—mark of stern respectability—were darkly green behind their guardian railings. An enclosed delivery van, of a sombre brown, showing on its sides in restrained lettering the name of a world-famous shoemaker, stood half-way along the Square. A string of glittering cars hugged the railings of the gardens. A maid in black and white came from a house and hurried away, touching her hair with one hand as she went. Except for the two men in charge of the restrainedly dignified delivery van belonging to the world-famous shoemaker, no one was in the Square.

The uniformed driver of the van on his throne behind the wheel called out impatiently to his uniformed colleague who was then shutting the door at the back. The colleague hurried round and, as the van shot forward, swung himself on board with the ease and beauty of long practice, and sank nonchalantly into his seat.

Then I noticed that someone else was in the Square.

A man in a dark grey suit was standing on the edge of the kerb near where the van had been. He was a fairly tall man, and his suit had the appearance of being a ready-made one.

I noticed these things, not because they were in themselves particularly noticeable, but because of the illusion of the man's having seemingly appeared from nowhere. In a moment, of course, I could see that he had been hidden by the van and that the moving off of the van had left him discovered. He started to walk slowly away.

I went up the steps towards my flat, and as I did so my mind flashed back to the Square as I had seen it last night—rather, early this morning—and I remembered the man who had come into it half a minute after I did.

Both that man and this man had a characteristic walk—the slow, large-gestured walk of the policeman.

I wondered what that meant.

My being unwittingly connected with so much that was mysterious made me assume at once that the presence of the policemen in the Square was due to me, directly or indirectly. Naturally I would assume that. That I knew myself to be perfectly innocent did nothing to alter my suspicions. I did not conclude that they were watching me, though, having regard to my being on intimate terms with two men who had met with violent deaths, I could not be blind to that possibility. For a moment, indeed, I thought that they could very well arrest me on suspicion, and my heart gave one or two uncomfortable thumps and I recalled a great deal that I had heard regarding miscarriages of justice.

But these were only startled fears. I had too much faith in the persistence of right to allow a foolish panic to grip me. If the police were suspicious of me, then they were suspicious of me. But I knew that as time went on they would not have reason to be more suspicious of me than they were now—unless another death among my acquaintances should occur, which heaven forbid! And they had not proved anything, of course; and they never would.

I was content, therefore, to let them watch me if they thought it their duty to watch me.

I ascended to my flat.

By this time I was weary from lack of sleep. I had not been to bed the night before, and in the meantime I had gone through some very intense nervous experiences. Yet I was determined not to give way to my extreme weariness, but to wait until night so that I should sleep soundly.

A strange young man—weedy and nervous—opened the door for me. This was another of my ancient retainer's staff.

"Makepeace about?" I asked, handing him my hat and gloves.

"He's lying down, sir. He isn't feeling too grand, sir."

"Oh, I'm sorry to hear that! Nothing much, I hope?"

"No, sir. Said he felt a bit tired."

I went to my study, through the door that opened directly out of the hall.

"A bit tired!" I murmured to myself, suddenly realizing the stuff that Makepeace was made of. "He hasn't slept for two nights, and he says he's only 'a bit tired'! I've missed only one night, and I'm dead beat."

In the bedroom, as I could see through the open communicating door, there was a new piece of furniture—a large, ungainly sort of settee. Makepeace's idea for snatching some rest during the night!

How reverently I thanked heaven for Makepeace!

I returned to the study and, selecting a book, threw myself into an easy chair. Mr. Ashton, I knew, had gone down to the City with some lists of investments that my solicitors wanted to look over. At four o'clock someone would come in with tea and a few slices of thin, rolled brown bread-and-butter. Makepeace awake or Makepeace asleep was equally reliable.

In the meantime I had two hours in front of me, a delicious sense of tiredness, and an entertaining book.

I read a page or two, and then I found that I was dropping off to sleep. I pulled myself together with a jerk and again fixed my attention on the book. But my tiredness was greater even than I had thought it to be. My eyes closed involuntarily and my head began to droop forward on to my chest. I got up and took a few vigorous turns about the room. And when I thought I had shaken myself fully awake I sat down again.

But my attempt at fighting against sleep was hopeless. I simply fell asleep. I did not doze off. I do not remember any period of gradual sinking into unconsciousness. I simply fell asleep. And in that room—the room into which the ghost had fled two nights before!

And what follows is the simplest account I can give of my experiences from the moment of falling asleep.

I knew I had fallen asleep. I mean that I was conscious of the fact that the young man, Martin Strange, was lying in that easy chair—his back to the window, his face towards the empty fireplace—asleep. I could see him. I could see his head slowly roll over sideways. I could see the book slipping bit by bit from his relaxing fingers. I could hear it fall to the floor with a cluttering of pages, and see it come to rest open and face downwards.

I was horribly afraid. The room and everything in the room was invested with the sinister significance of objects glimpsed in nightmares. Everything was hostile and deadly, charged with horror. Things that in daylight were innocent and that called forth pleasant associations had lost their passive characters and were transformed into symbols of active, malignant force. (For it was no longer daylight. Night had come. They had forgotten my tea. They had not called me, I remember thinking, but had allowed me to sleep on; and it had grown dark, and the terror had come forth.)

And though acutely, intensely conscious of the horror that was going on around me, I could not wake myself. I was in a fever of excitement because of the inertness of that body with the pale face lying peacefully sleeping in the chair.

I thought of it objectively. I feared for it. It was the other half of me—the physical half—and I was bound to protect it from the encroaching malevolent force that was in the room. I wanted to scream, and could not.

Then I became aware that out of the darkness and the encroaching terror two eyes were looking at me. They commanded me. I dared not let my attention wander from those eyes. They were the supreme horror in that room of horror. All the evil of the world seemed to be concentrated in those eyes, and all the evil was transformed into active hostility against me.

I knew I must meet that hostility and hold it at bay by a superhuman effort of will, or it would slowly envelop me and render me incapable of protecting the unconscious body in the chair. And the protection of that body was the sole reason for my existence. If I failed in that I should be overwhelmed and die, and death would mean endless terror.

The eyes came nearer and nearer, so slowly that they seemed hardly to advance. But they did advance, and they would continue to advance. They held me, fascinated me, made me impotent in my terror. Their expression was wholly and unbelievably evil. There was in them nothing of sympathy, pity, mercy—nothing that I could understand; nothing to which I could appeal. They were as the eyes of a snake, and my helplessness was as the helplessness of a rabbit. I felt myself forgetting all else but the bestial cruelty of those eyes.

Then a change came over the room. It was not my study, though it had the same sinister atmosphere. It was Christopher Knight's bedroom.

Christopher was there—alive. I knew he was there, though I could not see him. And someone else was there—someone I dared not face.

I knew—how I knew I cannot tell—that some terrible truth was to be revealed. And I could not bear to have that truth revealed. I would die before I should look at what was about to happen. Christopher Knight's murder was about to be enacted again, and I was to witness it so that I might know the identity of the murderer, who was that inscrutable presence whom I dared not face.

And I knew I must see it. I had not the power to flee. I had not the power even to look away. And I knew that if I were to see it the sheer horror of it would kill me.

But my will was not strong enough. I was now completely in the power of those sinister mysteries.

Movement was going on about me—stealthy movement; and it was Christopher who was in danger.

In an access of panic I shrieked. Panic gave my will a momentary ascendancy over that which had subjugated me; and the horror instantly fell away.

I opened my eyes to the familiar, comforting solidity of my study. In the easy chair at the other side of the empty fireplace sat Professor Wetherhouse.

CHAPTER XIV

A GAMBLE

"YOU MUST excuse me, old chap, for violating your privacy like this," said the Professor. "They tried to turn me away when they found that you were having forty winks, but I said I would wait."

"Forty winks, was it?" I said, struggling into a sitting position. "I'm glad you did wait. I was having a most horrible dream—an unspeakably horrible dream."

I put my face in my hands for a moment and screwed up my eyes as one does who tastes something vile and nauseating.

The Professor looked at me closely. I wondered whether he suspected that my experience had been something more than a dream. For it had been something more than a dream. Other personalities besides mine had been positively active in it. It had possessed the characteristics of nightmare, but it had possessed more than that. It had been a struggle between me and a conscious intelligence which had been determined to lay bare the secret of Christopher Knight's death.

"You were sleeping very soundly," remarked the Professor, looking at me, I thought, curiously.

"Have you been here long?" I asked, returning his gaze.

I did not hear what he answered. I rose quickly and took a few turns about the room. His gaze disturbed me. There was something about his eyes that made me afraid with the same fear that had possessed me during my journey into that other plane of consciousness.

"Tea will be through in a moment," I told him, eager to shake off the effects of horror, eager also to hide my uneasiness from him. "You couldn't stay to lunch at Lady Somerton's? I was sorry. I hope that you will visit us when we settle at Bolton Towers. It won't be long now—just over three weeks."

"Is that all?" he asked, startled I thought.

"Yes, three weeks to-morrow."

I was wondering whether he might be induced to say something on the subject of postponing the marriage. I didn't see how he could, but I could not resist the opportunity for giving him a reminder that if he intended to postpone the wedding he had better hurry up about it.

My remark, however, had no other effect than to make him sit silently for a few moments with a creased forehead.

Glancing at him, I wondered how he hoped to manage to have the wedding put off. There was only one way, so far as I Could see, and that was to approach Sylvia, to influence Sylvia in some way so that she might suggest having it put off for a time. Certainly they could not influence me. And I was very doubtful about their being able to influence Sylvia. It would be interesting to know what method they would adopt—rather, what method the Professor would adopt. Lady Somerton did not have the same convictions as the Professor had. She was anxious for the marriage to take place. She liked me—I knew that. She was not indifferent to my wealth and consequent social position. And she had no notion of what lay behind the Professor's restrained suggestions.

I was thinking that Lady Somerton would not go very much out of her way to do as the Professor had asked her to do. Yet, did she but know that I was in touch with the other world, and that I was living in the midst of indescribable horrors, she would shrink from me as though I had the plague. She would move heaven and earth to prevent my marriage to Sylvia. But she did not know, and the Professor dared not tell her.

But the Professor knew. I put myself in the Professor's place, and I asked myself what *I* should do were I to become acquainted with a case such as this. I could not but be honest about it. I knew that I should override everything—laws, social behaviour, and all the rest of it—in order to save such a charming girl as Sylvia—or any other girl, for that matter—from the horror of being married to a haunted man.

My duty, therefore, was to make a clean breast of it all, to tell the Professor that I knew what he suspected and that I knew that his suspicions were correct. But did I? Did I entertain the thought for one moment? No. What was right in the case of another, supposititious, man was definitely not right in my own case—which argument was according to the universal rule.

But the Professor would judge and act impartially. *He* would not be restrained by the fact that my love for Sylvia was to me the greatest thing in the world. He would think only of Sylvia, and would go to any extreme to prevent the marriage.

Surely the strictest judgment will not blame me for clinging to the one bit of happiness that was left for me in life! I had done no wrong. I was merely involved in wrong through the curse that had clung to my family throughout generations. I should have been more than human had I voluntarily forfeited my chance of happiness.

"What were you dreaming about?" the Professor asked suddenly.

I assumed as light a manner as I could. And fortunately the tea came in before I had time to answer. The man who brought it was in the room for a minute or two, arranging the tray on the table; and during that time I was able to collect my thoughts.

"Something about Red Indians," I said, smiling as I set about the business of pouring out the tea. "I really can't describe the dream. It was not dramatically coherent. There was plenty of atmosphere about it—of the usual sinister kind. But that was all. You take sugar?"

"Two lumps, please . . . About Red Indians, you say. It isn't often that people dream about Red Indians."

He was looking at me keenly. As I set down the teapot I glanced at him and surprised a look on his face that did not do me very much credit. I received the impression that he did not believe me. I coloured slightly. I was never one to carry through a deceit in a cool manner. But he had no right to question me on such a matter. Surely one's dreams were one's own!

"Well, this one *was* about Red Indians, whatever other people's might be about," I asserted, rudely perhaps.

I think that made him more inclined than ever to disbelieve me, but it had the effect of putting an end to the subject.

"I just looked in," he said, "to ask you about Ashton. I might have asked you at lunch-time, but it slipped my memory. However, I happened to be passing here this afternoon. How is Ashton shaping? Is he satisfactory?"

"He's wonderful!" I exclaimed. "He's saved his salary over and over again by dealing with matters that I should in the ordinary course have to submit to solicitors. He seems to know everything about everything. Where did you find him?"

"Oh, I've known him for a number of years now. I was sure he would be satisfactory; but I wanted to ask. I like to keep in touch with my—my protégés."

"He's a dab when it comes to legal affairs," I went on with enthusiasm. "And he's a bit of a doctor too. One of the maids dislocated her arm two or three days ago—slipped as she was going into the kitchen with a tray. I told Ashton to telephone for a doctor. But when I told him what was wrong, he went through and saw the girl himself. I don't know what he did, but he didn't telephone for any doctor, and the girl is as right as rain now."

"Yes," said the Professor, "I think he did study medicine for a while. Anyway, I'm glad to hear that he is to your liking."

He seemed disinclined to talk about Mr. Ashton's history, and I did not press the subject. But I was curious about Mr. Ashton. The man's unconscious manner made me think that he was someone of more account than a gentleman's private secretary. And his knowledge of medicine, which had been brought into use over the maid's accident, and his knowledge of law, which was frequently being brought into use, gave point to my opinion. And then there was the belief of Sylvia and her aunt that they had met Mr. Ashton before! All these things served to make me curious about him. But the Professor had said that this old friend of his was down on his uppers, and I contented myself with reflecting that it was quite possible for a man who had studied medicine and who possessed a smattering of legal knowledge to be down on his uppers, even though his manner was that of confident assurance.

The Professor left immediately after tea.

"Be sure to call again when you are passing," I said. "I am usually in during the afternoons. If I know that you have been in the Square and haven't called in I shall think that you don't care for my tea—and Makepeace goes all the way to the Strand to buy it."

I said that not merely out of politeness but because I did want him to call on me as often as he liked. I guessed he had called with the intention of finding out something—studying me, perhaps—exploring in those realms that were only vaguely understood, if they were understood at all. And I was content that he should do so. He would find nothing. At least, I should tell him nothing. But he might drop some accidental hint that might be useful to me. And he might bring up the subject of the postponement of the marriage.

It was as well to have him about me frequently, I was thinking. I should then perhaps be able to counteract any move he might make.

"You don't know what you're letting yourself in for," he re-plied, laughing. "I pass through this Square every day. So I take it that you want me to have tea with you every day."

"Good!" I exclaimed. "I shall expect you tomorrow sometime before four."

He and I, I could see, were both playing a game of deceit. I wanted him to call. I was eager that he should call, so that I might follow the workings of his mind and so that, perhaps, I might con-vince him by my behaviour that his suspicions were quite wrong. And he wanted to call. He was eager to call, so that he might study me. And so we both played this game of pretence, and he thought that the first trick was his.

When I returned from seeing him to the door, the manservant was gathering the tea-things on to a tray.

"I'm expecting Professor Wetherhouse to call to-morrow at about the same time," I said.

"Yes, sir," he replied, leaving the tea-things and standing up very straight.

"In fact, I think the Professor will be calling fairly regularly in the future—perhaps every day."

"Yes, sir."

"I want you to let him in without any formality. You under-stand. As though he were expected. As though he were one of the family. If I happen to be out, ask him to have tea. In any case al-ways show him into the study here. It's not likely that you'll catch me asleep again, as you did to-day, but if—"

"Catch you asleep, sir?"

The man looked at me in a quaint manner.

"You let the Professor in to-day, didn't you? Or was it some-body else?"

"I did, sir. Mr. Makepeace said that no one but me was to an-swer the door, sir."

"Well, wasn't I asleep when you showed him in?"

"*Asleep,* sir?"

"Man alive!" I exclaimed, beginning to be irritated by the fel-low's denseness. "Didn't you see me sitting in that chair asleep? *This* chair," I added, bringing my hand down on the back with a smack.

"Why, no, sir, I didn't."

"Not when you brought the Professor in?"

The man looked at me queerly, and took a step backwards.

I thought he was afraid because of the sudden impatience I had shown. He continued to look at me with the same puzzled expression on his face.

"Well?" I said at length. "Didn't you see me lying there asleep when you showed the Professor in? What's gone wrong with you?"

"Nothing, sir. Only, I didn't show the gentleman right in here. I only met him at the outer door, sir."

"Then who showed him in here?"

"Why—why *you* did, sir."

"*I?*"

As I said the word a wave of chilliness ran over me, and at the same time I broke out into a perspiration. The chilliness and the perspiration signified fear. For half a minute I was unable to speak. I could hardly reason. But I was convinced that the young fellow was telling the truth; and instinctively I was on my guard to prevent his scenting any mystery.

"Of course!" I exclaimed. "I let him in. I had dozed off, and I wasn't quite awake again when he arrived. That's right. I'm sorry for having contradicted you."

It was perhaps the first time he had ever been apologized to by anyone whom he addressed as sir.

"That's *quite* all right, sir."

When he had gone I paced the room, pondering over this fresh mystery.

My fear had given place to a kind of intense self-pity. I felt myself to be the tragic, non-comprehending innocent cast into the arena to be the sport of thoughtless tormentors. For their passing pleasure I was made to suffer the most inconceivable tortures. My sense of justice was outraged. Why should I be chosen? Why couldn't they leave me alone? No sooner was one act over than I must be dragged in again to be the victim in another!

But self-pity would avail me nothing. The way of self-pity was the way of self-destruction; and by too long dwelling on the injustice of my position I might be tempted to make my quietus "with a bare bodkin." And from that I shrank. I was little more than a youth: the greatest promises of life had not yet been fulfilled. And, besides that, I had a faith in the ultimate victory of right. I must not give in. I must face the position.

But the position, as I turned it over in my mind while I paced that carpet, was becoming more involved and less capable of being understood by a puny human intelligence.

The two deaths had seemed to follow some sort of a principle. Both had taken place as an apparent consequence of my wishes. If these two deaths had embraced the whole of the phenomenon then I should have been fairly easy in mind, knowing that I had only to guard against an excess of bitterness against anyone in order to avoid a repetition of the manifestation.

But the curse did not stop there. Makepeace's discovery of two nights ago, when he heard the unearthly sounds coming from my bedroom and saw "something" disappear into the study, showed that the power was now exercising its influence directly upon me. That it had failed then was undoubtedly due to Makepeace's intrusion.

And then to-day—the vividness of to-day's experiences still sent a shiver down my back. I had seemed to be an actual partaker in some ghostly business—a manifestation that defied the limits of time and place but which was, nevertheless, more vividly real than my everyday experiences. It was bad enough to have inexplicable happenings occurring in the world about one; but it was infinitely worse to be oneself the subject of such happenings. The ghost (I had to call it "ghost" for want of a less crude term)—the ghost had now settled its hands upon me. What it intended to do with me I could not imagine—I dared not try to imagine.

And the last disclosure of all—that was perhaps the one that brought with it the greatest horror.

That I should go out to the hall to welcome the Professor and that I should bring him into this room and thereafter know nothing about my having done so was to doubt my own identity—to doubt, indeed, my own sanity.

Then suddenly, while I was in the midst of the blackest conjectures about my soul being lost to those sinister forces who walked by day as well as by night, a flash of comprehension came to me.

So great was my relief that I hardly dared give way to it in case my theory might be wrong. I hardly dared to think of it, for it seemed too good to be true. I was trembling with excitement, but I steadfastly discouraged that excitement. Time enough for self-congratulation when I should have succeeded in proving that my suspicions were justified—in proving, that is to say, that the ghost that was putting its spell over me was less of a ghost than I had thought it to be.

I rang the bell. The young manservant appeared and stood just within the doorway.

"Is Makepeace about yet?" I asked.

Mr. Makepeace was not about yet.

"Well, you might call him now and tell him I want to see him. It's rather important."

The young fellow must have thought me rather an inhuman being, for he was under the impression that Makepeace was indisposed. I also wondered whether I was being unkind in rousing the old man from his well-earned rest. But I could not wait. Now that I was on the track of an important discovery, I could not rest until I had taken the first steps.

I paced the floor for an interminable time, then Makepeace appeared. My conscience ceased to sting me: he looked fresh and sprightly.

"I want you to go on a holiday," I said, when he had entered the room and shut the door behind him.

"On a holiday, Mister Martin?"

"Yes. To-day."

Makepeace was flabbergasted.

"But I haven't anywhere to go," he managed to stammer. "And what about to-night? I dursn't leave you here alone. They'll—they might kill you, Mister Martin. I dursn't do it."

"But you must do it. I wish I could explain to you just why you must do it. But it's too early yet. I might be wrong. I say, I might be wrong. But I'm going to stake my life—literally my life—on the chance that I'm not wrong. If I'm right you'll have no further trouble with midnight apparitions in *this* flat. If I'm wrong—well, you'll have no further trouble in that case either . . . I think I've discovered the reason for the disturbance two nights ago, and the reason for another disturbance to-day—though you don't know anything about that yet. But I would rather not say anything—just in case I'm wrong."

Makepeace had not recovered sufficiently to grasp fully what I told him.

"But if they come again when I'm not here!" he exclaimed.

"That's just why I want you not to be here," I hastened to explain. "I want them—or it—to come again. I want to give them—or it—every encouragement to come again. We have a revolver somewhere, haven't we?"

"Yes, Mister Martin. But no cartridges to it."

"Oh, well, never mind the cartridges. The revolver will do. If it's a real ghost, bullets won't be any protection against it. And if it isn't a real ghost, the sight of a revolver will do the trick . . . Nobody knows, of course, that you intended to sleep in my room?"

"Nobody, sir."

"Good! Well, take this money and go to a hotel somewhere, and stay there until you hear from me. Send me your address to-morrow morning."

"But," said Makepeace, with hesitation, "if anything should happen—I mean, if I shouldn't ever hear from you again—"

"Oh," I said, laughing, "I don't think we need make any plans to cover *that* possibility . . . Tell the others that you've been called away—somebody ill. And have a good time."

I was keenly affected by Makepeace's manner as he mournfully set about the business of preparing to have a good time. I ought to have explained my plans and suspicions more fully to him, for he certainly merited my fullest confidence. But, to tell the truth, I was half afraid that if he knew the risk I intended to run he might have definitely refused to leave me, and that would have ruined every-thing.

"Good-bye, Mister Martin!" he said, an hour or so later, when a taxi stood out by the kerb and a porter was carrying his case downstairs.

"Not 'good-bye'!" I said, smiling.

"Ah!" he murmured. "I'd better say it—in case."

CHAPTER XV

OUT OF THE DARKNESS

THAT EVENING happened to be a free one for me, and, after dressing, I wandered into the hall, trying to decide what to do with myself.

I could run round to Park Lane, I reflected; but I was not in the mood for going round to Park Lane. I was restless and impatient I wanted something freer and less personal than the atmosphere of Park Lane.

There was the club. I would be sure to find one or two pleasant sparks there who would do all that could be done in the way of making the evening pass quickly. I decided to go to the club.

It was then that Mr. Ashton crossed the hall.

"Are you busy, Mr. Ashton?" I asked.

"Why, no, sir. I have one or two things that—"

"Do you think you could leave the one or two things, and come with me to the theatre?"

"Certainly, sir."

Mr. Ashton would insist on the "sir." But perhaps, I reflected while I was waiting for him to dress, an evening of social intimacy would soften his austere formalness in that respect.

We dined at a restaurant, Mr. Ashton and I; and after dinner we strolled forth and took our seats to witness one of the most successful plays that was then running in London.

I found Mr. Ashton to be as great a success socially as he was secretarially; and I was glad that I had chosen to spend the evening with him. He had the supreme skill to keep the conversation away from "shop"—a feat that requires no little genius—and not once during the whole evening did he mention any of the hundred little matters that are continually crying for remark between secretary and employer.

He did, it is true, mention Makepeace; but that was not a matter of business. He had understood that my old retainer was ill, and was glad to learn that not only was he not ill but that he had gone away on a visit to someone who *was* ill.

Yes, Mr. Ashton was an accomplished social companion, besides being an accomplished secretary, and at odd moments during
the evening I wondered why I had not sought his company earlier.

But the main point was that the evening passed quickly and that
my mind was kept from dwelling upon the ordeal through which I
might have to go when I left the pleasant company of Mr. Ashton
and retired to my bedroom.

The time for retiring quickly arrived. And though I was eager
to be alone in order to test the correctness of my suspicions, I was,
at the same time, unwilling to part with the company of another
human being.

"We'll have a drink before we turn in," I suggested, as we
stood in the hall of the flat. "Come through to the dining-room for
a minute."

The dining-room was at the back of the hall. Its door was next
to that which cut off the servants' domain—next to that green
baize-covered door that was symbolic, in Makepeace's mind, of
the line of demarcation between master and man.

I remarked on that point to Mr. Ashton—not for the sake of
telling him anything so much as for the sake of expressing my own
fears to myself.

"Makepeace is the supreme autocrat," I said. "He has given this
door the virtues of a portcullis and a drawbridge combined. I understand that instant dismissal is the punishment should any of the
servants be found on this side of it after nine o'clock at night."

Mr. Ashton laughed. Somehow I could not bring myself to
laugh. Now that the time for retiring was so near, the confidence
that I had formerly felt began to diminish. There was something
profoundly significant in that green baize-covered door. It gave me
a sense of being apart from the rest of mankind, of going forth unattended to meet a foe of whose powers I was in total ignorance.

I might have told Mr. Ashton of my fears. I might have over-
ruled Makepeace's orders and had two of the menservants through
to keep watch. There was no physical reason why I should go
through with the grim ordeal that I had set myself.

We lingered a long time over our drinks. I was unwilling to
lose sight of the solid, squarely built figure of my secretary. My
confidence was oozing rapidly. What, in daylight, had seemed
comparatively easy and free from terror was now charged with all
the circumstances of doubt and apprehension. I had thought only
of the ninety-nine chances of success, and not at all of the one
chance of failure. But now it was the one chance of failure that

impressed itself upon me; for if my suspicions were wrong it meant that I was putting myself unreservedly into the hands of forces of whose intentions I had no conception.

"Good night, Mr. Ashton!" I said suddenly, putting down my glass. "Thanks very much for your company. It's been a delightful evening."

I dared not linger there, thinking over the possible outcome of my night's vigil. I walked determinedly through to my bedroom.

As I undressed I whistled. There was a steadying influence in whistling. The chief thing was not to give way to panic. If I allowed my thoughts to dwell on ghostly matters I would be done for. Terror, I argued, was a state of mind. There are some people so grossly equipped, mentally, that terror for them is a thing unknown. There are others so acutely sensitive to impressions that they start at a shadow. I, with nerves frayed through my recent experiences in the world of the supernatural, was one of these latter.

I must keep my thoughts on innocent, everyday things, I told myself. Will—that was the secret. The will to think of the prosaic, the commonplace. If my mind were occupied with other thoughts there would be no room for terror. Terror, I told myself again, was merely a state of mind.

I went over the plot of the play that we had witnessed that evening. I followed every detail of the first scene, and was surprised at the calmness that the exercise induced. I could walk about the room as coolly as though I were walking in the crowded street at midday.

The door leading into the study was shut. I strolled over and opened it, looking for an instant into the half dark interior. And I deliberately turned and came back into the middle of the bedroom. The slightest flicker of my strong hold upon myself would have caused me to wheel round and face that door, for it was through that door that the terror would come.

But—I cannot help saying it—I took pride in the manner in which I kept my back to the door. My casualness was sublime. So far, at least, I was master of myself. If I could retain that mastery I should have nothing to fear.

I switched off the lights. The room was in utter blackness. Then I walked to one of the windows and drew aside the heavy curtains. 1 even stood by the window for a time looking down into the Square. The sound of the midnight traffic of Oxford Street came to me in an uncertain murmur. The night sky glowed mysteriously.

Down in the Square—on the same side as I, but at some distance along the pavement—a man was standing. I smiled. He was
another of those who walk with slow, large-gestured strides. That
they were watching me—or, at least, someone connected with me
or with my establishment—I had not the faintest doubt. My smile
turned into an expression of seriousness. It was not a thing to
smile at, even though one is constrained to smile at the thought of
someone hunting for a mare's nest. All the tragedy and the mystery that had come within my knowledge since the fateful night of
my first meeting with Sylvia Vernon must, I thought, be traceable
to one single cause. Christopher Knight's death, my cousin's
death, my own weird experiences, the presence of the policeman
down on the pavement—that these all rose from the one funda-
mental spring I was certain.

Would the mystery ever be solved? Would I ever be rid of the
unearthly genius that was interposing itself between me and the
innocent cultivation of life's pleasures? Was I now about to solve
the mystery—or part of it?

I turned from the window and faced the darkened room. Objects in it were now visible by the faint glow that came from the
night sky. The room was just a shade less than intensely dark. My
nerves were already beginning to get the upper hand of me. I
turned my thoughts to the play at the theatre again, and, by an effort, kept them there. Meanwhile I got into bed.

I came, in thought, to the final "curtain." Then I started all over
again. I told myself that I must not allow my thoughts to wander
indiscriminately. They would lead me back to the present, if I did,
and I should find myself lying in wide-eyed anticipation of some
queer happening. I must keep them fixed on one set of circumstances that would call for my whole powers of concentration over
a considerable period. To review the play in detail was a perfect
exercise for the occasion.

It must have been about an hour later—when I was puzzling
over the manner in which one of the characters came up stage—
that I heard a sound in the study.

In an instant my sublime self-control vanished. I might as well
have been lying in shivering, fearful expectation all the time for all
the difference it made now that the supreme moment had come.

My useless revolver was in my hand. To Makepeace I had argued lightly that cartridges didn't matter. What a self-sufficient
fool I had been! A cartridge would at least arouse the household.

I ought to be feigning sleep and watching the door of the study through half closed eyelids. In bitter truth I was wide-eyed and was straining every nerve to pierce the gloom of the chamber.

After that first faint sound there was a deathly, sinister silence.

Then the blackness that was the oblong of the study door was disturbed. The blackness became less intense—seemed to mould itself into the rudiments of form. Something was evolving out of darkness. Something wraith-like was standing there in the door-way.

I could not move. I could only stare at the apparition standing motionless and silent, only vaguely distinguishable in the enveloping darkness of the room.

"Don't look at its eyes—if it has eyes," I told myself, grasping fearfully in my mind for some point by which I could retain my last vestige of self-control, and lighting, fortunately, upon a precaution that I had instilled into myself earlier. "Don't look at its eyes."

The apparition, vague as a wisp of fog in the darkness, seemed to be moving forward into the room. Yet the silence was unbroken. It seemed to move without effort. It had grown less indistinct. It was coming towards me.

I cannot say how I should have behaved had it continued to advance in that same stealthy, noiseless manner. Probably I should have swooned outright, for with every second I could feel the control ebbing from my limbs.

A board creaked. And with that sound the sense of control came back to my limbs. My tenseness relaxed. I found that I was breathing regularly, and that to feign sleep was no very difficult matter. "Boards," I told myself, "don't creak under the weight of wraiths."

The thing had advanced, as nearly as I could judge in the darkness, to about the centre of the room.

It was still only a shadow, and it still advanced with infinite slowness and without apparent effort.

I had become extraordinarily cool. That creak of a board had proved part of my theory to be correct, and though I was perhaps in some danger I was only in physical danger, and that was a comparatively small matter: bad enough, no doubt, but nothing in the light of my recent experiences in the supernatural world.

I let the figure approach a step or two nearer.

"Don't move!" I shouted suddenly, quickly. "Or I'll blow your brains out!"

At the same instant I switched on the light at the head of my bed, and jumped out, getting between the intruder and the doors.

"Mr. Ashton?" I said. "I thought it might be you."

And Mr. Ashton, in a dark suit and with the collar of his jacket folded over so as to hide the whiteness of his shirt, was too greatly surprised to make any comment. He just stood there, where my rather melodramatic words had arrested him.

But though he was startled he showed no sign of fear. He did not cower. Even at that moment, when he was caught in a situation the implications of which would make most of us take alarm, he showed the same cool self-confidence that had always marked his demeanour. There was nothing overbearing in his manner, but just the calm self-possession of a man who knew just where he stood in the world.

"What are you doing in here?" I asked.

His eyes were on my revolver.

"That thing might go off," he said.

"It might very easily go off," I answered. "What are you doing in here?"

"You wouldn't believe me if I told you."

"Perhaps I should. Shall we try?"

"No," he said, very deliberately; "we shan't. But you said you thought it might be I. What made you think that?"

It was characteristic of his natural forcefulness—that quality that he had tried unsuccessfully to hide while he was playing the part of secretary—it was characteristic of that that he should now become the questioner and I the questioned.

I ought to have refused to answer. But I was answering him before I knew what I was about. I had caught him in a suspicious position, and I had a revolver. These two points in my favour ought to have made me capable of doing anything I liked to do with him. But I could not do what I liked with him: his stronger personality made me, even at this moment, treat him with respect.

"You were the only other person in the flat besides myself," I said.

"Come, come!" he replied. "That's not true. You had other reasons. How do you account for the revolver all ready in your hand? Were you expecting me?"

I blushed. I, with a revolver in my hand, facing an unlawful intruder, blushed because of his quietly stated "That's not true."

"Yes," I said. "I was expecting you—you or Professor Wetherhouse."

"And why should you expect one of us?" he asked.

I was undecided whether to tell him or not. That I had expected him was not exactly the truth. I had merely suspected that these night alarms were due to physical causes: I had been prepared—at what risk I shuddered to think—to find them due to supernatural causes.

Mr. Ashton was not the man to give any information away. I might stand there for the rest of the night trying to trick him into making a disclosure, and the only result would probably be that I would disclose something to him.

Yet I thought I might as well put an end to some of the things that had been troubling me, so I said:

"You were disturbed two nights ago: I was sure you would come back. To encourage you I sent Makepeace out of the way."

Mr. Ashton, I think, was cursing himself inwardly for his stupidity in not having seen the trick.

"And I suppose," I went on, "I suppose you are wondering whether I know what you are up to—you and the Professor. I suppose you think I don't know."

I didn't know; but I had already guessed. I had guessed it when I was told by my young manservant that I had gone to the door and ushered the Professor into the study.

"You don't, Mr. Strange. And you never will know."

He spoke with a calm, professional assurance.

"You are trying to hypnotize me."

For an instant his easy manner left him. Immediately afterwards he was smiling, respectfully scorning the idea, assuring me that the suggestion was preposterous. But his smiles and his respectful scorn came just too late. I had seen his start of surprise at the neatness with which I had hit the mark. Nothing that he might now say could undo that lapse.

"Yes," I said, interrupting him, "you tried it two nights ago and you didn't get anywhere. Then the Professor tried it this afternoon and—and very nearly got somewhere. And now to-night—But you shan't try it again."

With that I crossed to the fireplace and rang the bell, keeping the button pressed for a considerable time. Then I threw the revolver on to the bed. It had served its purpose. Now that I was aware of their intentions neither this man nor the Professor could harm me.

And that I was aware of their intentions I had no doubt whatsoever. Mr. Ashton had not said a word in answer to my last assertions.

While waiting for someone to respond to my summons I took a turn or two about the room.

Mr. Ashton did the same.

He said nothing, though I have no doubt that he was in a perfect maze of bewilderment over my attitude. He must have been furiously asking himself how it was that I could take it all so calmly and why it was that I hadn't asked him to tell me the reason for the attempts at hypnotizing me.

But I didn't ask him, for I already knew. It was the Professor's method of causing the wedding to be postponed. He had put Mr. Ashton into my household with the primary object of inquiring into the supernatural matters connected with my family—of the existence of which he had somehow been made aware. They had not yet discovered anything, apparently (I was certain that they never would); but they had been trying to use their position to influence me, by hypnotizing me, so that I might have the marriage put off for a time.

I had guessed all this, and to-night's discovery had convinced me that my guess was not far from the truth.

There came a knock at the door, and it was opened by the young man whom Makepeace had apparently appointed his grand deputy.

"Help Mr. Ashton to pack," I said. "While you are doing it I'll telephone for a taxi."

CHAPTER XVI

A Statement of Policy

S PEAKING ABOUT Mr. Ashton," said Sylvia, when I recounted to her as much as I thought fit of the affair of the previous night, "do you remember I told you that he reminded me very much of someone I knew?"

"Oh, yes. You thought you had met him before," I remarked, trying not to appear too greatly interested, but moved by the liveliest impatience. "You've just remembered whom he reminds you of?"

"Sir James Lambert-Smith," she said.

"Sir James Lambert-Smith?" I echoed. "I've never met him, but he's a brain specialist, isn't he? Or a psychologist, or something of the sort?"

"Yes, something of the sort. It just occurred to me when you were telling me about your secretary."

So it was Sir James Lambert-Smith whose brains *I* had threatened to blow out with an unloaded revolver!

"You must tell Sir James that he has a double," I said, laughing. "You needn't mention unless you like that the double is something of a burglar."

I was in the highest of spirits. Sylvia and I were on the roof-garden of a Regent Street store. Lady Somerton was within the store, where we had left her inspecting curtains and proving that shopping is perhaps the one art in the world that women take more seriously than men.

I had been compelled to say something about Mr. Ashton, and had given Sylvia to understand that my promising secretary had turned out to be a common—or, rather, uncommon—thief. But I had treated the matter lightly. I was too happy to do otherwise. The fact that these last frightening phenomena had been explained—or had, at least, been brought down to a physical basis—was an unspeakable relief to me. That the Professor was on the scent of my secret I knew. And that he and his colleague—Sir James Lambert-Smith—had been trying to hypnotize me I also knew. Hypnotism had been resorted to, I imagined, with the idea of making me tell them what I knew about the family secret—though how they suspected the existence of any secret I could not guess. And they had probably been using their power, incidentally, to try to make me postpone the wedding so that they might have more time for their experiments. But all these things I did not mind.

My terror at the thought that the ghost was seeking to destroy me had been groundless. In that lay my sense of infinite relief. I could bear almost anything but that.

I could bear the knowledge that there was a curse upon my family, for I knew that, so long as I did nothing to bring that curse into action by allowing myself to be overcome by a fatal hatred of anyone, there would be nothing to fear. And 1 could bear the thought of the two deaths that had occurred, for though they were due to the mysterious shadow that seemed to hover about our house I was not personally responsible for them. And I could bear the scientific inquiries of the Professor. He would never find out anything now.

In short, life was a more pleasant thing than it had ever been—especially on that warm roof-garden with Sylvia on the stone seat by my side.

"Three weeks to-day!" I said. "We'll be in a pretty state of excitement by this time."

Marriage was apparently a matter more serious to a woman than to a man. Sylvia did not respond to my enthusiasm.

"Yes, three weeks!" she said; but I thought I detected a touch almost of regret in the exclamation.

"You sound as though you weren't looking forward to it," I remarked thoughtlessly.

"Oh, but I am!" she protested, turning her smile to me for a moment, and gripping my arm as though to emphasize her words. "Should I be marrying you if I were not looking forward to it?"

That was, of course, unanswerable.

How was I to doubt her protestations? How was I to imagine then that she loved not me but that shy young fellow, Sydney Wetherhouse? How was I to reason that it was Lady Somerton who had chosen me for Sylvia's husband and that Sylvia was not in a position to do otherwise than obey her aunt?

None of these questions touched me. I knew only that Sylvia Vernon, the most beautiful girl in London, was going to be my wife.

"What did Professor Wetherhouse say when you told him about that Ashton man?" she asked. "Have you seen him to-day?"

"No. I'm expecting him to look in for tea this afternoon."

"He'll be sorry to hear that the man he recommended has turned out so badly."

"Yes," I said, dryly. "He'll be very sorry indeed."

We got up. It was time to remind Lady Somerton that lunch was more immediately important than curtains.

As we descended into the comparative gloom of the store I was wondering what would be the future relations between Professor Wetherhouse and me. On account of his being a friend of Lady Somerton's I could not ignore him. I decided to be frank with him—frank in letting him know that I was aware of his having hypnotized me; but apparently in complete ignorance as to the reason.

What his next move would be I could not guess. If I had not overheard that conversation between him and Lady Somerton I should have been completely mystified over his recent attentions to me; but now I could take the fullest measures to guard my secret and to guard against his next move whatever it might be. I could not forget that in speaking to Lady Somerton he had shown how grave he considered the matter to be. He might take any steps to prevent my marriage to Sylvia.

Nevertheless, I was not troubled. I had a notion that in discovering the manner in which he was investigating my case I had put an end to these investigations. His job had been a delicate one—that of trying to find out, without my knowing it, the truth about the family ghost. He had chosen to worm the secret directly out of me instead of troubling to look up family records, assuming that any existed. But the job now would be infinitely more difficult, if not impossible. I had been forewarned.

The supreme mystery to me was how he had got on to the track of my secret.

But sufficient for the moment was the joy of being with Sylvia and, I might say, the joy of being seen with Sylvia. And as we stood craning our necks to catch a glimpse of Lady Somerton I was conscious of a number of glances, in our direction—glances caught first by Sylvia, taking in the exquisite beauty of her appearance, and then turned towards me as though to ask who I might be and how I came to merit the position of escort to such a ravishing companion.

But Sylvia, I noticed, was completely unconscious of these glances. Her whole mind was on the business of finding her aunt, and her eyes were on the distances along the aisles of merchandise. Her simple summer frock, of some flowered material, was mystically alluring because of its very simplicity. There was nothing ostentatious about her, nothing arrogant; yet she was the most compelling person there. That indefinable attraction that she had exercised upon me when I first set eyes on her was recognized by others also.

"Auntie doesn't seem to be here," she said at length.

"No," I said, suddenly attentive to the business in hand. "Shall we—where do you think she might be?"

"I don't know. We'll just wander round, shall we?"

So we wandered round, and found ourselves among the handbags, and then among the umbrellas, then the groceries, then the gramophones and radio.

"Curious!" said Sylvia. "She said she would wait for us where we left her."

We were making our way back to the curtains. We had come upon a palace of luxury—a floor crowded with settees and easy chairs.

"There she is!" I exclaimed; but instead of hurrying forward I stopped and detained Sylvia with a touch on the arm. Lady Somerton was at the other end of the showroom talking angrily to Professor Wetherhouse.

We went forward slowly.

Sylvia had smiled when I drew her attention to the two at the other end of the room, and had, no doubt, put my pause down to diffidence about interrupting a "scene."

Yet it was not the "scene" but the meaning of the "scene" that had startled me. The Professor's business must be very urgent, I thought, if he has troubled to come here in search of Lady Somerton.

"How d'you do, sir!" I said, as they both turned and saw us within a few yards of them.

Lady Somerton's attitude changed immediately. The flush that had been on her face died away. She was smiling as she welcomed us.

The Professor managed to raise a smile too; but it was a forced smile. I felt sorry for him. I could see that he had had the worst of the discussion that Sylvia and I had so abruptly ended.

"That man you recommended to me," I said after a moment or two—"he's an out-and-out bad lot. I found him breaking into my bedroom last night. He can thank his lucky stars he didn't get a bullet through his head."

I told them the story of the midnight prowler exactly as I had told it to Sylvia.

The Professor was extremely sorry at the thought of his recommendation turning out so badly.

"My dear Martin!" he exclaimed, and the ladies were, no doubt, taken in by his manner. "I should have trusted that man with my life."

I was sure that my news did not come as a surprise to him. I was sure that he had spoken to Sir James Lambert-Smith that morning, and that Sir James Lambert-Smith had told him that their experiment had failed. And I was sure that that was why he had sought Lady Somerton so urgently.

I was happier than ever, and was disposed to make some pointed remarks about the disappointing Mr. Ashton. Having failed on one side, he was renewing his efforts to influence Lady Somerton against the marriage. And Lady Somerton was refusing to be influenced.

"There are very few people," I said, "whom I would trust with *my* life. And after the scare I got last night I shan't be responsible for what might happen to the next burglar who disturbs me. Whether he happens to be a secretary or a plain guest won't matter a scrap. If I find that there's any funny business going on I'll shoot. Last night's affair rather unnerved me."

The ladies, of course, must have thought I was talking flippant nonsense. But the Professor, having had Sir James Lambert-Smith's account of what had happened and of what I had said last night, took my words seriously.

I had not originally intended to say anything like this. The opportunity presented itself, and on the spur of the moment I said what I thought might be most effective in discouraging further unwelcome attentions.

I watched the Professor's face as I spoke. And, as I say, I felt sorry for him. He knew that there was a mystery somewhere. Perhaps he knew more than I suspected him of knowing. He guessed, at least, that there was some supernatural influence at work about my life. He feared that that influence might affect Sylvia. Yet he was powerless.

He was right. I was in sympathy with him. I could understand his fears. Had these spiritual manifestations referred to anyone but myself, I should have been eager to help him.

Yes, I was sorry for him. Lady Somerton would not listen to his pleading. Her attitude must have exasperated him beyond measure. And now here was I stating that I would shoot anyone who interfered with me!

He shrugged his shoulders, almost with a sigh, I thought; and turned to leave us. His attitude was that of one who would say, "If you won't let me help you, then you must take the consequences."

"Shall I be seeing you this afternoon?" I asked, as he inclined his head to me at parting.

"About dropping in for tea, you mean?" he said. "I'm afraid not. I shan't be along your way very often in the future. I have had to alter some of my plans."

With that he was gone.

I was left to understand that he had washed his hands of the whole matter.

CHAPTER XVII

AN ECHO

SYLVIA AND I were married.

At the time, I am afraid, I had no thoughts for anything but my own intense happiness. I did not stop to ask myself whether I was doing right in taking Sylvia—or any other girl—as my wife. The immediate promise of rapturous happiness made me incapable of judging such a nice point. Perhaps it did occur to me at the time that I was not quite playing the game in allowing Sylvia to marry me in ignorance of the fact that she was marrying a man who was in league with the devil—for by that phrase must I describe the relations that I unwillingly had with that terrible silent power of the other world. I say it might have occurred to me to tell her that; but I could no more tell her than take my own life. It would have meant throwing away my chance of supreme happiness, and my instincts were as human as anybody else's.

At odd moments since, I have wondered whether it might not have been better for me to have given up my secret before I allowed her to become my wife.

Had I known what I know now! But I could not tell that the spirit would start into activity again so soon.

In fact, with the discovery of the Professor's plan to experiment upon me the intensity of my fears had vanished. It was a long time since the death of my cousin, and his death had marked the last manifestation of the power of the ghost. I reasoned that there might never be another manifestation of that power during my lifetime. It was natural that I should reason like that. I was not going to forgo present happiness because of the possibility of future woe.

I had not seen the Professor since that day when he had left us abruptly in the Regent Street store, though someone said that he had been at St. Paul's, Knightsbridge, to see us married. I was sorry that I had taken that rather conclusive way of telling him to mind his own business.

We spent our honeymoon in touring the Continent. Those weeks were the happiest of my life. Sylvia's manner was still that

of the distant goddess; but I could not read into her manner anything beyond an expression of natural reserve. I had ceased to feel
that there was anything lacking in her relations towards me. The
fact that she had married me proved that she loved me, and further
than that my speculations did not go. I had fallen in love with a
distant goddess, and I was quite content that she should remain a
distant goddess—a thing eternally mystifying.

My happiness was complete. Had I been one to be affected unduly by marks of popular esteem I should have had my head
turned in real earnest, for wherever we went we were treated with
the greatest honour. I found that Sylvia's fame as a society beauty
was not confined to London; and during our tour of the Continent
the only thing that troubled us was the difficulty of deciding which
invitations to accept and which to decline.

Then we returned to Bolton Towers.

Our way to Bolton Towers, in Hampshire, lay via London.
There was no need for us to touch London, but we felt that our
first duty on arriving in England was to call on Lady Somerton, so
late one afternoon we sauntered up the black and white mosaic
path in Park Lane and rang the bell.

Our visit was unexpected. We had intended to go straight on to
Bolton Towers, where everything was ready for us. Only that
morning we had decided to alter our plans, and on arriving in England I had telegraphed to Hampshire asking them to send the car to
meet the last train from London that night. I had not, however,
telegraphed to Park Lane. We thought our sudden arrival would be
a pleasant surprise to Sylvia's aunt.

Lady Somerton was not at home. She was not politely not at
home. She was actually not at home.

We said, of course, that we would wait.

I have lately begun to take notice of the way in which the most
innocent-looking events start trains of activity of the most vital
importance. I had always known, of course, that one's life is, in
the main, ruled by the most negligible accidents. A chance meeting with an old friend results in an introduction to a charming
girl—and one's whole life is altered. A sudden whim makes one
go down a certain street instead of down another equally conven-
ient street, and results in the chance meeting with the old friend.
The fact that one's watch is fast makes one walk to keep an appointment instead of riding, and one walks down a certain street
and meets an old friend and is introduced to a charming girl—and
one's whole life is altered because one's watch was fast.

I knew all that, but it was not until my wife and I called at Park Lane and found Lady Somerton not at home that I realized how powerful these accidents were.

We had been waiting in the drawing-room for perhaps ten minutes—Sylvia pleasantly excited at the thought of meeting her aunt again—when we heard another visitor in the hall.

The door of the drawing-room was opened, and, without any warning, Professor Wetherhouse was ushered in.

It was apparent that he had not known that we were there. His conduct at the Grosvenor Square flat still lay unexplained between him and me. He could not meet me without wondering what I suspected him of, and he could not explain all that had happened. Yet here he was—unexpectedly brought face to face with me.

Sylvia rose and went to him immediately. I followed.

I was sorry for the Professor. His intentions had been of the best. He was scientifically interested in a case of supernatural activity and probably his method of inquiry had been justified in his own mind. I had nothing against him.

I followed Sylvia with the intention of showing that my regard for him was as great as ever it had been despite the puzzling shadow that lay between us.

"And you must come down to our house-warming," I said, after the first exchange of commonplaces. "We shall be very sorry if you can't, eh, Sylvia? It will be the week-end after next. Can you keep that free to oblige us?"

Sylvia seconded my invitation. The old man looked from one to the other of us, and his face, which had been somewhat troubled, took on some of its normal serenity.

I had not shown by a single glance that I remembered what had passed; and though it was impossible for us to ignore the strange behaviour of both him and the pseudo Mr. Ashton, we agreed tacitly to gloss it over.

He accepted our invitation.

"And Sydney?" I queried. "Sydney will come too, surely."

I had to include Sydney. But I noticed that in this case Sylvia did not add her voice to mine. She turned, though in a perfectly natural manner, and wandered across towards the window, apparently looking to see whether there were yet any signs of her aunt.

"Yes, we must have Sydney down," I said, eager to show, I suppose, that I was pleased to forget all that had happened.

"Well, I can't say off-hand whether he'll be free or not," the Professor explained. "But I shall certainly convey your very kind invitation to him."

"Here's Auntie!" exclaimed Sylvia, running from the window out into the hall.

The remainder of the Professor's stay was made in an atmosphere of excited chatter.

But at the back of the excited chatter there was an element of disturbance. Between Lady Somerton and the Professor one could detect hostility. With us she was spontaneous in her expressions of delight at seeing us again, but towards the Professor she showed a certain coldness, failing to catch fire from any expressions that *he* might venture.

"You called to see me?" she asked him suddenly.

"I did," he replied. "Yes, I did call to see you, Lady Somerton; but—but it doesn't matter now. The pleasure of meeting these young people makes my business of no account."

"Is it the same old business? I thought that was all settled."

"Yes, yes. Never mind."

The Professor was anxious not to have his business brought to the fore at that moment. Sylvia and I were uncomfortable because of the hostility that Lady Somerton showed and which she made no effort to conceal. Her eye glinted as it caught the Professor's.

I could not help wondering whether the trouble between these two was the same as had existed before our marriage. Could it be that the Professor was still interested in me as a "case" worthy of investigation? He had failed to stop the marriage, and that, I had thought, would put an end to his activities. He could not undo the marriage. Was he still existing in hope of being able to verify his theories regarding the shadow that was on my house?

He took his leave very shortly afterwards.

Lady Somerton's eyes followed him to the door, then she turned to me.

"And now—about this house-warming party of yours . . ." she began.

"The Professor is coming, to begin with," I said. "And Sydney as well, I believe."

She looked at me in surprise.

"Sylvia, darling," she said sweetly. "Would you mind going and amusing yourself for ten minutes? I want to have a private talk to this husband of yours."

Sylvia, assuming, I suppose, that an aunt has the right to ten minutes' private conversation with her niece's husband, withdrew, looking at us with a quizzical smile as though wondering what pleasant mystery was afoot.

"Sit down, Martin," said Lady Somerton, when she and I were alone. "I want to tell you something."

Her manner was serious, almost nervous. I took a chair facing her.

"Did you ask the Professor?" she said, after a moment's hesitation. "Or—or did he ask himself?"

"Oh, I asked him," I said. "He would hardly ask himself."

"I'm not so sure about that. I've found him out to be a most interfering and a most persistent man. And he is very eager to get on an intimate footing with you. I understand that something happened between you—I don't know what—and that for a week or two before your marriage you didn't see one another. Well, since then he's been trying to get on the right side of me so that the trouble—whatever it is—might be overcome. He's got a suspicion—I haven't the faintest idea of what he suspects—that everything is not quite as it ought to be. He has begged of me to help him. He has almost gone down on his knees to me. He wants to be on good terms with you—that is as much as I can make of it at the moment. I told him that if he couldn't tell me what it was that he suspected I could do nothing for him. He says he daren't tell me. It's much too serious, he says. Have you any ideas about what he is driving at?"

"None whatever," I assured her, trying to appear mystified, and certainly feeling uneasy.

"All that I can make out of it," she went on, "is that he wants to study you or something of the sort. Perhaps there's something about you of scientific interest to him. We mustn't forget that he's a scientist, and that what he regards as of the utmost seriousness might be—"

"Yes, yes. I understand," I interrupted. "Probably it is nothing more than some scientific theory he is trying to verify." I was not eager to talk on this subject.

"I had intended to keep you apart," she went on. "If I had known that you were coming here to-day I should certainly not have allowed him to meet you. Why didn't you let me know you were coming?"

"We intended to take you by surprise."

"Well, you did that. But you have also given the Professor the very chance he wants. That's why I'm speaking to you now. He told me not to breathe a word to you or to Sylvia."

"So you take the first opportunity of telling us!" I exclaimed, smiling.

"Yes. I resent his manner. I don't like to feel that a relative of mine (How delightful to think of you as a relative, Martin!)—I don't like to feel that a relative of mine is being regarded as a 'case,' and that is what it appears to amount to. So I warn you. If he has any scientific observations to conduct let him conduct them openly. You don't feel like a patient who ought to be kept under observation, do you?"

"I certainly don't," I told her, with a smile that hid my uneasiness at learning that the Professor had not yet given up his investigations.

"Well, that's all," she said, rising. "I think the whole trouble is that the Professor is growing old. Perhaps he is becoming eccentric. I don't know. I don't like to doubt his good sense, but a lifetime of study might be affecting him in some way. Perhaps it's best to look at it like that. If I were to take his manner at its face value I should say that what he has at the back of his mind is a grimly serious matter. He gives one the impression that it is a matter of life and death."

Again I laughed.

"Shall we leave it at that then?" I said. "Let's assume that he is labouring under a delusion of some sort . . . But thanks for warning me. I shan't be startled should I find him surreptitiously examining me with a microscope."

We went in search of Sylvia, whom we found standing with her back to the empty fireplace in the library intent on one of the morning newspapers which she held wide open, her arms outstretched.

When she heard us, she let the paper fall to the floor and buried her face in her hands.

We stood stock still at this unexpected sight. In an instant she recovered herself again.

"Why don't they leave him alone?" she demanded. "Why don't they forget about him, and let others forget?"

"Leave who alone?" said Lady Somerton, puzzled, as she went towards Sylvia and took her by the shoulders.

"Christopher," said Sylvia, in a voice that suggested angry tears. "Why must they rake it all up again? Will it matter to me—

to us who knew him—whether they ever find the murderer or not? Anything for a sensation! They never stop to think of *our* feelings. The—the ghouls!"

She buried her face on her aunt's shoulder.

I stood by, feeling rather helpless in the circumstances. It was hardly a moment for pointing out that the murder of Christopher Knight would rightly be kept alive in the public memory until the law should have done its very utmost to find the murderer.

As she continued to sob—unduly moved, I thought, by a memory that ought by now to be dulled—I stooped and picked up the sheets.

The item that had caused this outburst was an article which recapitulated some of the recent unsolved crimes.

About the murder of Christopher it said:

"Then there was the murder of the young man, Christopher Knight, in his rooms in Jermyn Street. This case affords an illustration of the obsolete laws that hamper the police. We were told some months ago that they were on the track of the murderer. We are told to-day that they are still on the track of the murderer. And that, if we reason from past experience, means that they have their man but dare not arrest him.

"We do not suggest that third-degree methods should be employed in this country, but—"

I folded the paper carefully and placed it on the table.

"Some journalist trying to turn an honest penny," I said. "Don't let that upset you. You may be assured that we shan't have to go through the ordeal of knowing that someone is being hanged because of Christopher's death."

"But someone ought to be hanged for it," asserted Lady Somerton, forgetting for the moment that the chief thing to do was to pacify Sylvia.

"True," I said. "But think of our feelings—even though it might be justice. However, the affair is too old now. The police are bound to say something to cover up their failure, so they say they are still on the track of the criminal. I bet they never catch him."

CHAPTER XVIII

THE APPARITION

A ND WHY IS this called Sir Osmond's room?" asked young Wetherhouse as I led him to the window of the bedroom that had been allotted to him at Bolton Towers.

I was about to point out to him the magnificent view that was to be had from that particular window, but his question stopped me.

"It used to be occupied, long ago, by someone of the name of Sir Osmond," I told him. "He was a grandfather of a cousin of mine. Come and see the view."

He came forward to the window, and for a few minutes I was occupied in pointing out the various features of the landscape to him. The window is high up in the West Tower and commands what I suppose is one of the finest views in this part of the country, looking, as it does, down five miles of thickly wooded valley towards the sparkling sea beyond.

But young Wetherhouse was not interested in the view. His mind was still on the name by which the room was known.

"Yes, it is delightful," he agreed, glancing casually out towards the sea. "But what were you saying about this Sir Osmond? What did he do? Why should the room still be called after him? Tell me if I'm being too curious, but this old place has caught my imagination, and if there are any legends connected with it—"

"The story of Sir Osmond isn't old enough yet to have become a legend," I told him. "It isn't even a story," I added, thinking I must be careful not to say too much or I might put this young man's father on to the right track for finding out the truth. "It isn't even a story because it has no dramatic shape. It's only an incident."

I was wondering whether Sydney was in his father's confidence. It might be that the Professor had detailed his son to find out anything that was to be found out about my family history.

I had barely seen the Professor since his arrival along with the bulk of the week-end guests earlier on in the afternoon. But I had no doubt that I should be seeing quite a lot of him. Lady Somerton's disclosures to me on the day of our arrival back in London showed how determined the Professor was. I was wondering what method he would adopt in the renewal of his inquiries.

"Tell me about it," said Sydney, with his youthful smile.

"But you are going to sleep in the room," I answered, taking a grim sort of pleasure in the expectation of making his hair stand on end, "Perhaps I had better not say anything until you are leaving. If you knew the truth perhaps you wouldn't want to sleep here."

"Oh, don't be afraid of that!" he exclaimed. "I don't—I don't believe in ghosts, if that's what you mean."

"That is just what I mean," I told him. "This room is supposed to be haunted."

A wave of mischievousness had come over me. "If they want to hear something about ghosts," I said to myself, "there's no reason why they shouldn't. Do they want data on which to base their investigations? Right! I'll give them something to be going on with. I can invent dozens of stories about ghosts. Anybody can. There's no need to give chapter and verse in stories about ghosts, for nobody can prove or disprove them."

"Is it really haunted?" he asked, and, despite his assurance of a moment before, his face became serious.

"Yes," I went on, my face as serious as his. "So, at least, the story goes; and there's usually some foundation for such stories."

"What is it haunted by? What's the ghost like?"

"That I can't tell you. It hasn't appeared during my lifetime. But, of course, the room hasn't been occupied as far back as I can remember. In fact," I added, glancing at him to see how he was taking my remarks, "it hasn't been used since Sir Osmond was killed."

I hoped I was not being indiscreet. But I reasoned that at this distance of time Sir Osmond's death, in so far as it was an instance of ghostly activity, had almost passed into the realm of legends. In any case I did want to give these investigators—Professor Wetherhouse and his son—something to think about. I had no fear of their ever finding out anything of value.

"Since Sir Osmond was *killed!*" echoed young Wetherhouse, rather alarmed.

"Yes. He was thrown out of the window," I said, with a conscious air of indifference, as though such happenings were everyday matters.

"Oh!"

"That's what they say," I went on. "Of course, it doesn't follow that the throwing was done by a ghost. But certainly nobody ever found out by whom the throwing *was* done. And then there was a case before Sir Osmond," I told him, beginning to bring my imagination into play—"a solicitor of the name of Watkins. In the days of the stage-coaches, you know. Called on business. Wild night. Didn't relish the thought of the journey back home, so stayed the night. Slept in this room. Last sleep on earth."

"You don't say!" exclaimed young Wetherhouse.

"That's right, according to what has been handed on from one generation to another," I said as I turned to leave him. "You'll find your way down when you're ready, won't you?"

"But do you mean," he said, detaining me, "that no one has slept in this room since Sir What's-his-name?"

"That's right. You see, the past generation was more superstitious than we are. Nowadays we don't believe those old wives' tales. Why? Do you want to change your room? If you do, just say the word."

But it was daylight, and though he was affected by what I had told him, his moral fear was stronger than his physical. He was afraid to admit that he was afraid.

And, for my part, I did not blame myself for playing upon his susceptibilities.

The room itself had no peculiar power. It was associated with tragedy only in the matter of Sir Osmond Garway's having "met his death through the window. He might have done the same through any other window in the building. As a room it was perfectly innocent. The story about the solicitor, Watkins, was merely an imaginary piece of corroborative detail, as was the statement that the room had never been slept in since Sir Osmond's death. I didn't know whether it had been slept in or not.

But if they were on the look-out for ghosts, I thought I could not do better than put them into the frame of mind best calculated to make their investigations exciting.

I should not have troubled to recount this interview with young Wetherhouse were it not for the fact that it has had a most disturbing sequel.

It is now Saturday morning. At odd moments during the past month or two I have been writing this manuscript and now I have brought it up to date. Whether it will ever see the light of day I do not know, but the facts round about which it is written are of profound interest—at least, to me—and there has been a certain inevitability in the events that has caused me to think that a crisis will come sooner or later and that the mystery will be explained.

Most of the guests retired early last night. All the ladies did, at least; and by half-past ten a handful of us men were finishing the evening in the billiard-room.

I was not playing. And the game that was in progress was not being taken seriously by anyone—not even by the two players, whose shots were constantly being interrupted so that they themselves could add something to the conversation.

In the midst of this pleasant winding up of the day I noticed that young Wetherhouse was missing. The thought of him took my mind back to the afternoon when I had tried to make his hair stand on end with stories of the haunted room in which he was to sleep. I suddenly felt sorry for him, and thought it would be a kindness to go up to his room and see how he was faring.

Accordingly I slipped out of the billiard-room and went up the main staircase and then along various corridors and up various smaller flights of stairs until I came to the West Tower.

As I went I was thinking that perhaps I had gone too far in my attempt at scaring the young man. The number of dim, echoing corridors that had to be traversed before the West Tower was reached were sufficient in themselves to give one a feeling of uneasiness, and when one's sensibilities had been sharpened and one's fears set on edge by stories of the supernatural, one would have to be brave indeed to face a night in that isolated part of the mansion with equanimity.

I intended to tell him that we had changed his room—that is, if he had not yet gone to bed. It was only because the place was very full that Sir Osmond's room had been brought into use; but I had no doubt that another empty room could be found even at this time of night. The ghostly atmosphere of the corridors was beginning to get on *my* nerves. With every second I was becoming more and more sorry for young Wetherhouse.

His room was empty. I knocked first, and received no answer. And then I opened the door and switched on the light. A mere glance around the apartment showed that he had not yet come up to go to bed.

I switched out the light, and was shutting the door again, when I thought of the window. The window of that room has been of tremendous significance to me ever since Makepeace told me of the sixty-year-old tragedy.

It was thrown right up, as it had been that afternoon. And, so much had I been affected by the isolated position of the room and by the eerie corridors and by the stories that I myself had told about the place, that I could not help looking out to see that everything was in order. I do not know whether I expected to see young Wetherhouse's body lying inert on the gravel below, but I know that I did look out and was relieved to see that no accident had occurred.

For a moment I stood surveying the calm, mysterious, moonlit valley that stretches away towards the sea, and then my attention was attracted to a movement on the edge of the lawn below.

Two figures were coming towards the house. They were partly hidden from my sight by the overhanging branches of some trees that grew from the edge of the gravel, but I could see that they were a man and a woman, and I could also see that they were strolling along very close together.

I was about to withdraw, for it was no business of mine that some of our guests should do their courting out in the moonlit grounds; but I was held spellbound to my post, for at that moment the couple stopped and turned and faced one another, and I could see that they were Sylvia and young Wetherhouse.

They were talking. At least, Sylvia was talking; but only the soft murmur of her voice reached me. Then I saw Wetherhouse look at his watch and turn as though to come across the gravel towards the house. But Sylvia gripped his arm and detained him for a further half minute, and there continued to reach me that soft murmur that was so maddeningly indistinct.

I do not know what I thought. But at that moment a thousand little impressions came back to me—impressions of Sylvia's coldness towards me—a coldness that I had thought to be part of her undemonstrative nature—impressions of her lack of enthusiasm over our marriage and our future, impressions of a quickening of her interest in the presence of that young man to whom she was now talking.

I could hardly contain myself. Perhaps it was fortunate that I was separated from them by such a height, for in the first shock of seeing these two together in such a position of familiarity I could think of only one thing—the utter destruction of both.

I turned from the window and flew downstairs. I did not go by the main staircase, but by the winding and rarely used stair within the tower, deciding instinctively to take the shortest way down.

But the journey was not so short but what I had time to put some sort of a check upon myself. What I had seen had every appearance of a secret intrigue between these two; but the truth was that even in the midst of my tumultuous thoughts I was seeking for some other explanation. Had the affair concerned anything but the love of Sylvia I should probably have simply given way to the dictates of impulse and settled the matter summarily. But when it touched Sylvia's love for me my whole nature rose up against my accepting the evidence of my own eyes. I did not want to believe what I had seen.

By the time I had reached the bottom of the old stairway and had unbolted the heavy door that gives out on to the gravel Sylvia and Wetherhouse were ascending the steps towards the hall. They were walking apart now and were conversing with every appearance of aimless innocence.

I did not show myself, but waited until they were both well within, then sauntered round to the front door. By the time I reached the hall they had both disappeared. I assumed that they had gone upstairs; but chancing to look into the billiard-room I found young Wetherhouse had joined the company there.

"Seen my wife?" I asked him, with as much casualness as I could command.

"Why, yes," he replied, with a frankness that quite disarmed me. "She has just gone to her room."

"Did she find it cold outside?"

He looked at me in surprise.

"Out on the lawn," I continued, and was about to tell him what I had seen, when we were interrupted by one or two of the group who wanted me to take a cue.

I excused myself. I wanted to have this matter settled without delay. But before I could say a word to prevent it young Wetherhouse had accepted a challenge to play a hundred up for a pound, and I had to chafe in silence for, disturbed as I was, I could not raise a to-do in the presence of so many of my guests.

I left the room and dashed upstairs to the bedroom occupied by Sylvia and me.

She was standing by the window when I entered. The wrap that she had been wearing lay at her feet where it had fallen from her shoulders.

At my entrance she turned, gave me that polite smile of hers that seems to hide so much more than it reveals, and turned again to her contemplation of the scene without.

I was tempted then to say nothing. Perhaps I was imagining more than had actually occurred. To suggest in cold words that she was being false to me would be to destroy all the happiness that I had. If she were not being false, my accusation would be an unforgivable insult. If she were being false, a word would set her on her guard. I had felt all along that I had not the power to hold her. She was my wife because she chose to be my wife. I was her husband because I had come under the spell of her wonderful beauty; but with her, I had always felt, the marriage had been one of the head rather than of the heart. And, that being so, I hesitated to speak.

"Sylvia," I said at length, "was that you I saw out under the trees with Sydney Wetherhouse?"

"Yes," she said, without turning round.

There was a pause. I looked at her back, which was bare almost to the waist.

"I didn't see *you,* " she said, still without turning round.

"No, I don't suppose you did," I remarked. "I was up at one of the bedroom windows. Don't you think it was rather—rather indiscreet to stroll about the grounds with one of the men guests when most of the others were in bed?"

She did not answer.

"Especially arm in arm," I added.

Still she did not answer.

"Would you care to tell me," I went on, my voice coming with an effort, "what you were talking about? You seemed to have a lot to say."

She turned then, and though we had almost the breadth of the room between us I started back a step.

Her face was a deathly white. Her eyes were keen and hard with the intensity of her feelings, and they looked at me with such piercing scorn that for the moment I was utterly aghast.

"I was telling him how completely miserable I am: that's what I was telling him," she spat out at me. "I was telling him that I had been put up in the market to the highest bidder, and that the highest bidder happened to be that self-satisfied popinjay, Martin Strange. That's what I was telling him."

"Sylvia!" I exclaimed, shocked and astounded.

"Don't deny it!" she said, pointing at me, her face now turned to an angry pink. "You've questioned my behaviour. Now I'm going to question yours . . . You wormed yourself into my aunt's favour—wormed yourself in like the despicable being you are—and made her agree to our marriage. Don't say you didn't! There was no word about marriage until the day your cousin died. You asked me at a time when I wasn't myself—when I was suffering from the shock of your cousin's death. Then you kept me to my word. Or you made my aunt keep me to my word, which was more despicable. You knew I had no money of my own. I couldn't defy my aunt . . . You must have known I didn't care for you. I have never taken any pains to hide the truth. You must have known it . . . You insisted on buying me. And my aunt refused to admit the sordidness of it. She said you were a very good friend to me when Christopher died. A very good friend! You did nothing more than any other man would have done. But a person like you *would* presume upon a favour of that sort. It wasn't until you came into your wretched fortune that you spoke seriously to my aunt. And then my aunt couldn't resist the temptation. One of the wealthiest men in England!"

"Sylvia! Sylvia!" I cried, interrupting the torrent of bitterness. "You're out of your senses. I assure you that there's no truth in anything you say. I assure you that I have acted throughout with the most scrupulous honour. I had no idea that you were being forced into the marriage."

"Scrupulous honour!" she exclaimed, her tone of scorn more triumphant and more bitter than before. "Was it an instance of scrupulous honour when you stood listening outside the door of the little study in Park Lane? Don't try to deny that, because I saw you. And I saw you tip-toe back into the hall and make out that you had only just arrived."

"But Sylvia!" I began.

"So much for your scrupulous honour!" she went on, silencing me by the very force of her anger. "Then you took me abroad, and I hated every minute of it. Your wealth found us plenty of friends, and they flattered me and petted me because I was the wife of one of the richest men in England. And you spent thousands of pounds on me, and every pound was an insult. You thought—"

"But Sylvia!" I said, trying to stop the flow of bitterness.

I don't know whether I fully realized the meaning of her words. I was too greatly amazed by this sudden outburst to feel the desolation that I was soon to feel.

"Don't keep on saying 'But Sylvia!'" she exclaimed. "You question my conduct. You have the insufferable impudence to ask me whether I think it discreet to walk in the grounds with one of our guests. If I had known you were watching—spying—I should have given you something to watch. For now that it is all out I

don't care. I've had to consider my aunt. But now I don't care
what she says. And I don't care what people think. Sydney asked
me to marry him. Soon after you asked me. But my aunt wouldn't
hear of it. Sydney isn't one of the wealthiest men in England."

I strode across the room and gripped her by the wrists.

"Now listen to me," I said. A sudden surge of blind anger had
welled up within me. I was irritated beyond all patience by the
unjust things she had said. I wanted to shake her, to force her to
believe that I was one of the last to think of taking advantage of
the accident of wealth in a matter of love, to prove to her that she
had misjudged me.

Her extraordinary beauty was never shown to better advantage
than at that moment. It was enhanced by the spirit that flashed
from her eyes. It made her more desirable than ever before, and I
felt that I must convince her of her error and of the honourableness
of all my actions.

She did not shrink. She stood stolidly defying me; yet not altogether defying me, for now her anger had subsided, the hot flush
had left her face, her eyes were lowered to the ground.

"You're hurting me," she said quietly. "Don't hold so tightly."

I dropped her wrists. She turned, took a step or two across the
room, and sat down at her dressing-table. She was her old unemo-
tional self again, and as I watched her marshalling the various
brushes and gold-capped pots and bottles, my thoughts were on
her extraordinary capacity for self-control.

But for the accident of my seeing her and young Wetherhouse
from that upper window I might never have known a tenth part of
what she had spat out at me. And all these months she had kept her
feelings under control. That was a staggering thing to realize. She
had caught me eavesdropping, and she had never given a hint of it.
Her opinion of me—mistaken though it was—could hardly be
lower; and yet she had hidden it all. Circumstances had forced her
to accept me, and she had accepted me. And she had kept everything locked up behind that coldly beautiful exterior until a word
from me had broken through her reserve and the whole bitter truth
had come out.

"You have completely misjudged me, Sylvia," I said, speaking
to her reflection in the glass.

"I think not," she said, calmly unscrewing the cap off a bottle.
"In any case, I don't want to hear what you have to say."

"But that's unfair," I retorted. "If you will let me explain—"

At that she got up and wheeled about quickly, her hands clenched shoulder-high, her face the incarnation of outraged patience.

"Oh, go away!" she screamed. "After what I've told you how can you ask me to listen to you? Go away! You know the truth. And all your explanations will not alter the truth."

Yes, the truth. That was the only thing that mattered. It was of no moment whatever that she should have misjudged me. The only thing that mattered was that she loved somebody else. All the talking in the world would not alter that.

It was then that the full sense of my desolation came to me.

There was nothing more to be said. I walked backwards away from her towards the dressing-room, and every slow step I took was an irrevocable step away from the object that I loved before everything else in the world.

I did not speak. I could not speak. I was dazed by the unreasonable cruelty of it all.

In the dressing-room there is a couch. I looked at that couch. That was the bed to which I, the husband of the celebrated Sylvia Vernon, was reduced.

I sat for a long time in a state of uncomprehension before I started to change. I was not immediately capable of realizing the full force of the blow I had received.

Curiously enough my feelings were not directed against young Wetherhouse. I hardly thought of him as being responsible for what had occurred. And did it matter whether he were responsible or not? The outstanding fact was that Sylvia had come to dislike me with a fierce, unreasonable dislike. All my feelings were directed against her, against her injustice, against the obdurate fact that all argument was futile.

In the night I awoke, and sprang up from the couch.

I had lain for hours trying to grasp the full bitterness of all I had learnt, but at last I had fallen asleep. And suddenly I was wide awake again and was through in Sylvia's room before I realized what was afoot. So startling was the summons that had aroused me that I do not actually remember getting off the couch.

Sylvia was crouching against the wall at the farther side of the room in an attitude of the most abject fear. The moonlight coming through the window showed her up clearly—showed even the fearful expression in her wide-open eyes.

She was silent now, but I knew that her shrieks had awakened me. I could still hear their echo in my brain.

I was by her side in an instant, and had lifted her on to the bed, where she suddenly burst into a most violent fit of crying.

By this time one or two of the others in the house had been aroused. I could hear voices in the corridor outside, and then there came a tap at the bedroom door.

"Are you all right?" asked someone.

"What's the matter?" said the voice of the Professor.

"Sylvia, darling!" pleaded Lady Somerton. "Whatever is wrong? May I come in?"

It seemed that everybody in the place had been aroused.

I looked at Sylvia. She was trembling from head to foot. I had never seen anyone in a fit of hysteria, but I guessed that that was what was the matter with her. Her hands were working incessantly—covering her face at one moment, clutching her throat at the next. Her weeping continued, violent and unrestrained.

"Why don't you let them in?" she suddenly demanded of me.

"But what's the matter?" I asked. "What happened?"

She did not answer, but threw herself over on to her face, her sobs now becoming cries.

I switched on the light and opened the door. A crowd of startled faces greeted me.

Lady Somerton pushed past me, followed by Professor Wetherhouse and Dr. Grainger whose room was almost opposite. There was no need for them to ask my permission to enter. My face, apparently, showed that this was no time to stand on ceremony.

Dr. Grainger immediately took the case in hand. He did not waste time in questioning Sylvia just then, but by some means best known to himself he succeeded first in pacifying her.

This took some time; and it was while I was standing apart that there first came to me a horrible suspicion.

The scene with Sylvia earlier in the night and the utter deadness of spirits which had followed that scene had driven my mind away from that weird power that had twice in the past taken a hand in the control of my affairs. But now the look of horror in Sylvia's eyes recalled a similar look that I had seen on the dead face of Christopher Knight. I was trembling. I dreaded the moment when Sylvia should be able to speak and give an account of what had happened, lest her words should confirm my awful suspicion.

Dr. Grainger turned to me, and spoke in a low voice, glancing from time to time at Sylvia who was now clinging to Lady Somerton and staring, with an expression of horror, into space.

"She's had a terrific shock of some sort," he said. "What happened?"

I told him that I didn't know. I said that I had been sleeping on the couch in the dressing-room, that I had not felt like going to bed and had lain down on the couch to read for an hour or so, had fallen asleep and had been awakened by her screams. Even at that moment, when it almost seemed to me that Sylvia's sanity was in the balance, I had to conceal the real reason for my being in the dressing-room.

He returned to Sylvia and tried to induce her to lie down.

But she would not. She shuddered as she glanced at the pillow. And suddenly she exclaimed, "Oh, it was horrible! Horrible! The wickedest face I've ever seen!"

"You were dreaming," I said; but I knew that she had not been dreaming.

I saw the Professor glance at me. I wondered what he suspected. If he were on the trail of the ghost, as I believed him to be, then he had struck the trail at a most fortunate point. Here was first-hand phenomena ready for investigation.

"Possibly!" said the doctor. "Though I hardly think a dream would put one into this state. You say you saw a face. Was it the face of anyone you know?"

She shook her head.

"Oh, no! It was too horrible. It wasn't a *human* face. I can't imagine a human face so—so bestial!"

"You were dreaming," I said again; and again I saw the Professor glance at me.

"It was close to mine," she went on, with a shudder. "And I know I wasn't dreaming," she added angrily, looking at me. "I could see the room—and I could hear the clock ticking."

"Well, well; never mind!" said Dr. Grainger. "Don't worry about that now. Tell us in the morning. You'll be better then."

I said I would sit with her; but she insisted on having her aunt to keep her company. She asserted that she would not sleep any more that night.

So we left them—Sylvia, Lady Somerton, and a maid who had unobtrusively appeared and who was saying something about tea when the Professor and the doctor and I went to join those who were still doggedly waiting in the corridor.

Later, I wandered through to this room that I call my study. Sleep was not for me. My mind was in a chaos. Desolation, fear, mystery! For the sake of my own sanity I sat down to add this further chapter to my manuscript. Only by forcing myself to set my mind to some intellectual work can I hope to keep from brooding.

And heaven knows I have enough to brood over!

I have lost Sylvia. And, as though that were not enough, the ghost has come back.

Undoubtedly my promptitude saved Sylvia's life. But what of to-night and to-morrow night and all the other nights?

I am of half a mind to tell everything to the Professor.

CHAPTER XIX

THE PICTURE

SATURDAY EVENING. Dr. Grainger and the Professor tell me that they intend to sit up with Sylvia to-night. I could say nothing against that, for Sylvia is in the doctor's hands and I cannot, without offence, object to whatever measures he cares to take. And I must act with a great deal of tact, for I believe that they are on the point of unearthing the family secret.

I ought, perhaps, not to care whether they do or not. If I have lost Sylvia nothing else matters; but the utter despair of last night has given place to a grim hope that I might yet get her back. I refuse to accept defeat—and I have had another defeat to-day. Perhaps, in a day or two, she will think better of me. When she is more herself she must see the tremendous injustice that she has inflicted upon me; and though I cannot expect to force her to love me I can still hope to induce her to live as my wife. I don't mind humbling myself. I don't mind playing on her pity. So long as I retain her the means do not matter. With that hope in my mind, therefore, I am as eager as ever that they should not find out about the family curse, for if they should discover that I am in league with the devil—for that is what it amounts to—there will be an end of my hope. And without hope there is nothing.

I made it my business to have a few words with young Wetherhouse after breakfast this morning.

Breakfast, after the disturbance in the night, was a rather haphazard affair. The time-table was ignored by half the guests. It was easy, therefore, for me to take young Wetherhouse aside without interfering with the programme of the day.

I brought him through to the study here.

On the way we met Sylvia and Lady Somerton just coming down. Both the ladies were showing signs of sleeplessness, but Sylvia had apparently recovered from the shock of last night.

The doctor had advised her, Lady Somerton told us, to spend the forenoon in bed, but that she had absolutely refused to do.

"Oh, I must be up and about," said Sylvia. "I'm perfectly well. They are talking about my having seen a ghost. What rubbish!"

"But you said so yourself, my dear!" said Lady Somerton. "You said so last night."

"Oh, I'm not responsible for what I said last night!" Sylvia exclaimed. Then she turned to me and added: "At least I'm not responsible for what I said after I woke up."

Lady Somerton laughed.

"But we quite understand that you were responsible for what you said before that!" she remarked.

Of course, Lady Somerton could not know that Sylvia's apparently unnecessary reference to what she had said before she went to bed was intended for me—was intended to show me that she was still of the same mind regarding me.

Perhaps there had been something in my manner that had made her think the reminder necessary. But though the glance that she gave me as she and her aunt turned towards the breakfast-room was far from encouraging, I was not going to be forced to give up hope until I had had a further talk with her and had fully stated my case.

Nevertheless, that chance encounter outside the breakfast-room made me all the more eager to settle this young fellow Wetherhouse once and for all.

I ushered him into the study here, and made the dramatic gesture of turning the key in the lock.

"Now, young man," I said, when I had asked him to sit down, "you and I have a piece of very personal business to discuss. I want to know what you and my wife were doing out in the grounds last night."

I think I have said before that young Wetherhouse is one of those *negative* people who go about completely at the mercy of their environment. He is extremely well-behaved, extremely honest, wholly inoffensive. He is a mirror of text-book perfection in these matters. But I doubt whether he ever did anything original in his life. He is content to follow the rules laid down for behaviour in a drawing-room, but one would never expect him to take the conduct of life into his own hands. It had been a very great surprise to me to find that it was he who was sharing in Sylvia's indiscretions.

"We were talking," he said.

"I know that," I told him. "But what were you talking about? That's what I want to know."

"And if I refuse to tell you?"

He said that very forcefully, but I could see that he was startled and afraid of me.

"I shan't let you out of here until you do tell me," I said.

"Now don't be silly!" he exclaimed, fingering his cigarette in a manner that showed him to be uncomfortable. "If your wife chooses to confide some of her lesser affairs to me, it's not my fault, is it?"

"That's the attitude you *would* adopt," I said with a sneer. " 'It's not my fault, is it?' " I mocked. "But it's your fault that you listened to what she had to say. And, in any case, she wouldn't say what she did say without encouragement. So she told you that she was unhappy, did she?"

That made him give a start.

"Now why should she tell *you* that?" I questioned.

"I'm sure I don't know," he said. "Unless it might be that I once asked her to marry me. Perhaps she thinks that gives her some sort of a claim on my sympathy—if she wants sympathy. That's the only thing I can think of."

"Did you speak about your having asked her to marry you?"

"Well, as a matter of fact, we did."

"What did you say?"

"I refuse to tell you."

Now that we were into the heart of the matter he spoke with some spirit. But I was not discouraged by his blank refusal.

"You were suggesting that the offer of marriage might still stand—if circumstances should ever make that possible," I hazarded.

"No," he exclaimed. "That was the very thing I was trying to discourage."

"Ah!" I said. "So *she* was suggesting that the offer might still stand!"

He was silent. I knew I had hit upon the truth.

I could have killed him where he sat. I had no doubt that he was perfectly innocent in intention. Or, rather, I was sure that however much he loved Sylvia he would never be able to pluck up the courage to overstep the bounds of convention in order to get her. I had nothing to fear from him. He would never rob me of my wife. Yet he was the man whom she loved. It was surprising that a girl of Sylvia's vital personality should love such a negative character as young Wetherhouse, but it was nevertheless true, and that was the fact I had to deal with. While he was alive I could not hope to influence Sylvia towards me again.

Had I not spoken last night she might never have been prompted to disclose her feelings and we might have gone on living a life of make-believe—to me perfectly satisfactory make-believe—indefinitely. Young Wetherhouse would never take an active part in any disruption. But now that the matter had been brought out into the light Sylvia would not go back to our old footing.

Thus I reasoned as I sat facing the man whose silence was condemning my wife—the man who, though his intentions might be of the most honourable, had actually robbed me of the society of my wife. It was nothing to me that he was not taking advantage of his position. He was not vital enough to do that. But it was something to me that if he chose he might take advantage of his position. Sylvia, I knew, now that the whole affair had been brought out into the open, would not hesitate to go beyond the bounds of convention if he agreed to go with her.

So I could have killed him where he sat.

I never thought I should be glad to know that I was in league with the devil, but I was glad at that moment.

My whole instinct was to spring on him and send his soul to perdition; but I restrained myself. I tried not to think of him as the man who had robbed me of all the exquisite joy that was associated in my mind with the idea of Sylvia. I tried not to think of that, for I knew what the result would be if I were to let my jealousy run riot. But it was of no use. I could not possibly keep down my bitter hatred of him. The most I could do was to prevent its showing in my face.

I know that young Wetherhouse will die—as Christopher Knight died and as my cousin died. I am not responsible. I cannot stay the fulfilment of the curse. If the curse—or the ghost that Sylvia saw last night—operates with consistency, then I am sure that young Wetherhouse is ordained a victim, for he has come between Sylvia and me. Nobody who has come between Sylvia and me has escaped. Even Sylvia herself, when she flouted my love, aroused the ghost.

"Thanks for telling me so much," I said, forcing myself to appear calm. "I see that it isn't your fault. You have nothing to reproach yourself with—nothing at all."

I rose as I spoke. He followed my example.

"I'm glad you look at it like that," he said.

"It's the only way one can look at it," I told him. "I can't blame you for being in love with my wife. Forgive me for any disparaging things I might have said about you—the heat of the moment, you know."

The words came smoothly enough. I had sufficient control of myself to realize that I must not quarrel with him. For if he were found dead following a quarrel with me it might result in my being suspected of the crime of murder.

I did not hear what he said in reply. My mind was turned to a fresh aspect of the case. I was asking myself if I were not a murderer in effect. Should I not warn him of his approaching doom? Could I allow him to go to bed in that isolated part of the building knowing that he would be dead in the morning?

Yes, I could. I have done so. He has been in bed an hour at this moment when I sit here writing.

For the greater part of the day I have been worrying over that question. Yet I have done nothing. There is nothing that I can do. I warned him yesterday afternoon that the room is haunted. That will have to serve.

I cannot explain the whole thing to anybody. People might not believe me, it is true. But if they do believe me they will shut me away—they might even destroy me—for society would never allow a man with such power as I possess to be at large. I can do nothing.

There is one thing I can try to do. I have tried it, but without success. I have tried not to feel jealous of him. Counsel of perfection! As well might I try not to feel hungry or thirsty. The mere passing thought of Sylvia's beautiful eyes and the bitter reflection that the light in them is not for me but for him—that is enough to send the blood whipping through my veins and arouse the primeval instinct to kill.

I have not told even Makepeace.

When we came out of the study I waited in the hall, after learning that Sylvia had not yet finished breakfast. I had not to wait very long, but when she reappeared she was accompanied by a number of kindly disposed but inquisitive people who were eager to have first-hand information about the ghost.

Nevertheless, I succeeded in getting her aside, when I peremptorily demanded half an hour's private talk with her. She probably knew that she must, sooner or later, listen to what I had to say, unless she intended to cease all communication with me forthwith. She agreed to listen.

Meanwhile we had strolled upstairs to the first landing and

there I opened the door leading to the picture gallery, which was the one nearest to my hand, and led her in.

She walked some way down the long chamber and then, stopping, turned to me and said, "Well?"

Her manner was anything but encouraging, but I was not affected by that. I was affected only by the tremendous fascination that she exercised over me. Her reputation for being one of the most beautiful girls in England is not by any means a false reputation. And she reaped a further attractiveness from the fact that she was quite unaffected by her reputation.

She stood in the centre of the floor, stolidly waiting for me to begin; and I could only look at the exquisiteness of her figure in its grey sports skirt and jacket, and feel with every moment a more insistent desire to advance the two paces that separated us and take her in my arms.

But at length I began to speak. There is no need for me to repeat what I said. I pleaded my case as though I were pleading for my life. I was, indeed, pleading for something that is more to me than my life. I denied that there had been any suspicion of a conspiracy between Lady Somerton and me. I protested that I had never thought of throwing my wealth into the scale in favour of my suit. I told her that I would immediately relinquish everything I possessed if it were to mean that I might still have her. I explained the reason for my having listened outside the door when Lady Somerton and Professor Wetherhouse were talking together. I said that I happened to hear the Professor asking Lady Somerton to stop our wedding. That, I suggested, was a sufficient excuse for listening.

But, throughout the whole of my energetic appeal, she stood stonily unaffected. She could not doubt my sincerity. She could not but be aware of the unfairness of all she had said against me. But she did not retract one word. There are none so blind as those who do not want to see.

"And what do you propose to do now?" I asked when I had finished my appeal and she remained mute. "You're not thinking of running off with that spineless youth, are you? For one thing he wouldn't have the nerve to run away."

She did not answer. She was staring past me, apparently determined not to give me the satisfaction of hearing one word of comment pass her lips.

"If you expect me to arrange a divorce," I went on, "then you are going to be disappointed."

I wondered why I troubled to touch on the future.

I knew that young Wetherhouse's death was imminent. Still she did not answer. Still she continued to stare past me, her eyes concentrated on one spot.

"Sylvia!" I exclaimed. "Do you hear me?"

Apparently she didn't. Ignoring me, she took a slow step forward towards the spot at which she was staring. Her body was bent forward and her eyes had taken on the look of terror that I saw in them when I found her crouching by the wall in the bedroom.

I wheeled round quickly to see what was affecting her.

"That's the face!" she exclaimed, pointing to one of the portraits. "The face I saw last night!"

She turned to me and clutched me wildly. She clung to me and buried her face on my breast. The matter that had brought us here was forgotten.

"That's Mad Roderick," I said, looking at the picture—a comparatively small and very old oil painting of one of my very early forebears. "That's Mad Roderick, and he's certainly enough to give anyone bad dreams."

But, though I tried to speak lightly, I was almost as deeply affected as she was. I had never thought of assigning to the ghost the personality of one of my own ancestors. Here was a further step in my knowledge, but I was strangely shocked by the revelation. So it was the spirit of Mad Roderick that was walking the earth, I thought, seeing in this discovery of Sylvia's the link that might finally enable the Professor to arrive at the truth.

"Now don't be silly, Sylvia," I said. "You were only dreaming. You know you were only dreaming."

I could feel her trembling in my embrace.

"I said I was," she sobbed. "I said that afterwards. But at the time I knew I wasn't dreaming. It was too real."

"No, no," I persisted. "You must have seen this picture—perhaps without noticing it particularly—and the expression of the face has become lodged in your memory. And you dreamt about it. That's all."

Still clinging to me, she turned her head and looked again at the picture.

It is, as I had told her, a picture that is enough to give anyone bad dreams. There are no authenticated records about the original of the portrait, but enough may be learned from the painted expression of the face to allow one to build up a picture of the character behind it. Though the features follow the very marked lines that have characterized every member of our family, the individual expression in the case of Mad Roderick is that of sheer insanity. How the portrait came to be painted I do not know. The artist is unknown, but I can imagine that he must have been in very hard straits before he accepted the commission to paint the picture that now hangs in the gallery there. I can imagine, also, how Mad Roderick must have taken a diabolic delight in distorting his face so as to express the most bloodcurdling idea of insanity.

Such is the picture we both stood staring at.

"But," said Sylvia suddenly, "I *couldn't* have seen that picture. I have never been in here before. When you showed me round we just looked in at the door. I said I would wait and see the pictures later."

I could say nothing to that. My assertion that she had been dreaming last night could not be substantiated.

She was still holding on to me. Her face was white. Her expression was one of uncomprehending horror.

Unfortunately my horror was not so intense as hers. I was becoming used to the idea of the ghost. At least, I had got over the horror of my first acquaintance with the shadowy forces of the other world. There was something that affected me more intensely even than the unmasking of Mad Roderick. I had Sylvia in my arms. That was a greater fact than any other, for it had been to win her that I had borne so much horror in the past.

"I'll have the picture destroyed, and so put an end to your nightmares," I said, inconclusively. "And meantime I'm waiting to hear what answer you are going to give me."

That broke the spell, restoring her to the present. Realizing that she was clinging to me she struggled to break away. But I held her firmly, pressed her to me, and forced her face up to meet mine. It was madness, of course. I might have known that the girl who had spoken to me as she had done last night would not submit to such treatment. But I could not let her go. I kissed her again and again, while she struggled wildly to free herself. Then she broke away, and fled from the room, leaving me staring after her.

Then I turned and looked at the portrait of Mad Roderick.

And there was something in the wild, leering eyes of my ancestor that inspired me with an unholy confidence. Mad Roderick was on my side, I told myself. Mad Roderick would know how to defend the dignity of the family of Strange.

That happened this forenoon. I have not spoken to Sylvia since. It was unwise of me to let my feelings get the upper hand of my discretion—not only because it has widened the breach between Sylvia and me, but also because it has kept me partly in the dark regarding what is happening.

I spent the greater part of the day with the guests. A party of us motored over to the golf-course this afternoon. We had tea there, and did not arrive back until it was almost time to dress for dinner. Before we set off, however, I happened to be on the staircase when Professor Wetherhouse, accompanied by his son, came out of the picture gallery. I presumed that Sylvia had been telling the Professor about the picture, and went forward to see whether he had any theories to give.

He did not enlighten me, however. He spoke about the pictures generally, but gave no hint that he knew anything about the episode of Sylvia and Mad Roderick. Yet I am sure that he knows about it. The few words he spoke seemed forced. He was relieved, I think, when I joined the golf party.

After dinner to-night the Professor and Dr. Grainger called me aside and said that they proposed to keep an eye on Sylvia during the night. The doctor told me that she is in a very nervous state. If I would find another room, he said, so that I should not be in the way, they would be very greatly obliged. Sylvia must be kept under observation.

I agreed to that, of course. The Professor, though he was trying hard to appear calmly professional, could not quite hide his excitement. I know that he thinks he is about to discover what he has been looking for all these months.

It is about three o'clock in the morning. Everybody in the place has been in bed for hours, except the Professor and Dr. Grainger and me.

Those two are sitting on a sofa outside Sylvia's door. I am down here in my study writing up this account. It is the only thing I can do to keep my agony of mind from getting the upper hand of me.

The doctor has been down twice to beg me to go to bed. I have had practically no sleep for two nights, yet I dare not go to bed. At any minute something might happen. Either Sylvia or young Wetherhouse might be attacked. With that expectation on my mind I can hardly expect to sleep. Yet there must be a limit to physical endurance.

CHAPTER XX

THE VIGIL

I, THE PROFESSOR WETHERHOUSE who is mentioned in the foregoing pages, have been asked to add my remarks to the extraordinary manuscript in which Martin Strange has related his uncanny experiences.

I became interested in Strange and his affairs soon after the death of his cousin. In common with everybody else, including Strange himself, I was struck by the coincidence of the two violent deaths occurring within the one social circle; and as the case promised to be one that might yield to the special knowledge that I could bring to bear upon it I undertook its investigation.

My close association with those who were most intimately affected by the two deaths was the principal reason for my going into the affair; but it happened that the person in charge of the official investigations knew me and knew of my association with Lady Somerton's household, and in this way I was drawn into the case as a semi-official investigator.

The police at that time were actually suspecting Martin of being responsible for the death of Christopher Knight. They soon admitted to me, however, that their suspicions were based on nothing more than the coincidence of his being closely acquainted with Christopher Knight and with the other man, Michael Strange, who had met his death by falling over the highest gallery of the block of flats in which he lived. In other words, they were at a loss and were reduced to keeping their finger on the one person whom they could in any way connect with the murder.

I told them that they might as readily suspect Sylvia or Lady Somerton or me or Martin's old servant, Makepeace; and there I left the matter so far as my working in co-operation with the police was concerned.

I had already formed a theory of my own, based on sundry observations which it is unnecessary for me to mention in detail here; and I was surprised on reading Martin's manuscript to learn how nearly he himself had come to discovering the truth of the whole affair.

He mentions, I see, the occasion on which I met him in the Park a few days after the death of his cousin. It was then that I was put fairly on the track of the solution of the mystery. His manner during the few moments in which I spoke to him made me suspect that he was trying to hide something; and I find from his manuscript that it was then that he first began to suspect me of making inquiries into the affair. I do not, of course, blame him for that: it was quite natural for a man placed as he was to do all he could to hide the terrible truth that was slowly dawning in his mind. To be a haunted man is bad enough, as we may suppose; but to have it known that one is haunted is undoubtedly worse, putting one, as Martin states so often in his manuscript, beyond the normal, pleasant associations with one's fellows which provide so much of the happiness of existence.

I was fully in sympathy with him. By allowing the terrible truth to become known he would most certainly lose Sylvia, and that, as we have seen, was, in his mind, the supreme tragedy. He was ready to face a life of horror—to live in momentary expectation of some further tragedy—rather than give up Sylvia.

That brought up the first difficulty that I had to try to overcome. Unless I had his co-operation I did not see how I could proceed very far in my investigations. If my theory were correct I could prove it only by inducing him to open his mind to me or else by some fortuitous happening such as might never occur.

I quickly saw that there was no chance of his ever confiding in me, so I cast about for some way whereby I might force him to tell me what was in his mind. It was a matter of the most extreme delicacy, for a false step on my part would put him on his guard and there would then be no chance of my discovering anything.

I discussed the matter with my friend, Sir James Lambert-Smith. The case interested him very keenly, and he was ready to spend a considerable amount of time on it.

In fact, Sir James was prepared to forego his holiday abroad in order to assist me in my investigations, and we hit upon the plan of installing him in Martin's household in the capacity of secretary—under the name of Mr. Ashton.

Our intention, failing any event that might guide us in our investigations, was to hypnotize Martin and so get the truth from him. We have already seen how our efforts in that way ended in failure, though there was a time when I was within an ace of having my suspicions confirmed. That was the time when I, at my wit's end because of the fact that Sir James's operations had been discovered by the servant Makepeace, made one reckless attempt at hypnotizing Martin.

I should certainly have succeeded in that instance but for the tremendous resistance that he unconsciously put up. If I had only been able to gain his confidence and to assure him that by putting himself into my hands unreservedly he might free himself of the shadow that hung over him, all might have been well. But he was determined to keep his secret—or, rather, not to share his thoughts with anyone—and I could not bring myself to give him an assurance to which I myself could not fully subscribe.

My efforts at solving the mystery had failed, and I was cast back on the merest hope that some chance occurrence might put the key into my hand. I had got into Lady Somerton's bad books over my interference—though I do not blame Lady Somerton for that—and I was forced to see Sylvia married to a man who, through no fault of his own, might plunge her into a life of the utmost horror.

Then I found myself at Bolton Towers, where I was an actual witness of the tragedy that was (for who can question the decrees of Providence?) apparently necessary for the solution of the mystery.

I have not thought fit to alter Martin's references to my son. These were made at a time when Martin was suffering from an intense bitterness towards Sydney, and I let them stand because they show something of the emotional atmosphere that was essential to the fulfilment of the tragedy.

Martin has already given a full account of what happened on the Friday night.

On the Saturday forenoon, just before lunch-time, I met Sylvia on the staircase. At first glance she was her usual calm self; but when I stopped and spoke to her I could see that she was in a highly emotional state, and, thinking it might be due to the rather terrifying experience she had had in the night, I told her she ought to have taken Dr. Grainger's advice and stayed in bed.

She ignored that suggestion altogether. She said it was not what had happened last night that had upset her, but the fact that last night's happenings had been given a horrifying significance by what had happened that morning.

She then took me into an unused room and told me about the picture that she had seen—the picture of Mad Roderick.

I was inclined to pooh-pooh the idea that there were any ghosts about the place, but I nevertheless went up with her later in order that I might see this picture for myself.

The picture is all that Martin states it to be. There can be no questioning the insanity of the original of the portrait. As I looked at it, with Sylvia half cowering by my side, I was prepared to believe almost anything; and I did indeed think it not impossible that the spirit of Mad Roderick might wander abroad in the night, so intense was the evil force that lurked behind even the painted features.

I did not, of course, voice these thoughts. I was very grateful to Sylvia for having told me so much, though I hardly knew how the knowledge would help me; but I made out that she had been dreaming, for I knew I should do no good by telling her that she had not been dreaming; and, having reassured her as lightly and pleasantly as I could, I finished up by saying, "So that's what upset you to-day—the sight of a face painted on canvas?"

Then she told me that it was not only that; and thereupon she proceeded to give me an account of all that had passed between her and her husband, both on the previous night and in the picture gallery that day.

I did not attempt to check her. I was greatly distressed to learn that the marriage had so quickly broken down; and I was constrained to put in a word or two for Martin, for I knew that he was not deserving of the bitterness that she showed towards him. But it was useless to try to influence her then. Her bitterness was perfectly unreasonable. I listened interestedly, however, for it seemed to me that 1 should learn more from an account of the relations between these two than I should learn from any amount of prying into the family history.

The fact that my own son was the cause of the rupture gave me more than a moment's uneasiness; and when Sylvia had finished her recital—glad, it seemed, to pour out her troubles to someone—I asked whether there had ever been anything between her and Martin's cousin.

She looked at me in surprise; but I begged that she might tell me the truth, adding that I should think none the less of her for having carried on a light flirtation and that the truth in this small matter was of the very highest importance in helping me to prevent a repetition of the "dream" she had had on the previous night.

She told me that she had certainly been amused by Michael Strange's manner and that she was almost sure that he had been interested in her; and as she spoke I blessed myself for having chanced to alight on this out-of-the-way point.

Prompted by me she told me that she had noticed how Martin resented his cousin's arrival on the field, and she mentioned that it was at the first opportunity after the cousin's appearing that Martin proposed to her.

All this coincided exactly with my own theory, and after seeing Sylvia downstairs I went in search of my son and asked him what, if anything, had transpired between him and Martin during the two days that we had been at Bolton Towers.

He told me everything, almost exactly as Martin himself has related it—the story of the haunted room and the interview that the two of them had behind the locked door of the study.

Sydney was inclined to laugh at the idea of a haunted room; but I warned him not to scoff at things that we do not understand. I could not yet tell even him what was in my mind, and when he asked me why I said such a thing I replied that during the past day or two my views on certain matters had been altered considerably and that I was now very much inclined to believe in the existence of ghosts of a sort.

"If I were to tell you positively," I said, "that that room of yours is haunted, would you sleep in it? Would you sleep in it to-night, if I asked you to?"

He did not reply at once. I was glad that he did not. His reply, when it came, would not be the mere froth of bravado. He considered the question, looking at me meanwhile to see whether I were serious. I was intensely serious.

"Yes," he said; "but not for the fun of it. Do you think it is haunted?"

I told him that I thought it was.

"And," I added, "if anything unusual is to occur it will be almost sure to occur to-night."

I do not claim for Sydney that he is braver than the next man, but it is at such times as these that a man's real character comes out. Were he not my own son I should perhaps allow myself to say more on that point. As it is, I shall content myself with stating that though he actually turned a shade paler on hearing my words he did not say that he would decline the bed.

"Yes, I want you to sleep there to-night," I said. "You might get a scare; but remember that there will be somebody at hand. You won't come to any harm."

When I had finished with Sydney I went up to the picture gallery again.

I studied that extraordinary picture for a good while, fascinated, I must say, by the sheer depravity that was so well depicted in the cast of the features and that had been caught miraculously in the glint of the eyes.

It was by no means a caricature. The longer I looked at it the more evident it became that the work was a work of real genius. There was life in it. In fact, when I drew myself away from it and wandered round the gallery, picking out and studying the rest of the family portraits, I could see that that of Mad Roderick was the most "living" piece in the whole collection.

But I saw something else. I saw that all the portraits of those who had the family blood in them were easily recognizable by a certain indefinable expression.

I went back to Mad Roderick. Yes, it was there too. Despite the revolting disfigurement of the face the expression common to all the others could be seen.

I left the gallery with a fresh conviction that my theory was correct.

The household retired fairly early that night. Before twelve o'clock everybody was in bed except Grainger and me, who had settled ourselves on a sofa outside Sylvia's room, and Martin, who had said that he wasn't in the mood for bed and who was in his study on the floor below.

The first hour of the vigil passed quickly enough.

Grainger and I had everything in common, and we found enough to talk about. But soon our minds began to be distracted by the atmosphere of expectancy. It is one thing to approach a problem in a purely academic frame of mind: it is quite another to find that a point has been reached where the problem transcends the purely academic and becomes the personal, affecting the investigator not as a problem but as an emotional experience. Thus it was with me as the minutes lengthened. My mind, after the first hour, was concerned not so much with whether my theory would be proved as with the immediate atmosphere of the house. My sensibilities had become acute. The long, silent passages grew sinister in my imagination. The idea of the sleeping house and us two old men waiting there to see whether Death would creep forth out of any of the dark shadows was enough to try one's faith in purely scientific knowledge.

I rose, saying I would slip up and see how Sydney was faring. It was a longer and a more intricate journey than I had thought it to be; but I found the room at length.

At the door I called softly because I did not want to startle the boy by going in without saying who I was. He did not answer. I opened the door quietly and glanced inside. He was sleeping peacefully if somewhat noisily. It was evident that his fear was not so great as his physical needs.

On my return to Grainger he reported that nothing had stirred.

After another half an hour Grainger thought he would go down and see whether Martin were yet thinking about going to bed.

He came back with the news that the young man was busy writing.

Another hour passed. By this time we had taken to walking up and down the corridor.

Again Grainger went down to the study. Martin was still writing, but Grainger said that he looked as though he would fall asleep at any minute.

That was the minute we were waiting for. I was intensely excited. I did not know what would happen. At the bottom of my heart I hoped that nothing might happen and in the same instant I hoped that everything might happen. My reasoning told me to look to Martin for the solution of the mystery—for the solution of all the tragedy that had touched those about him since his introduction to Sylvia.

His temporary bedroom was in the corridor in which we were waiting. We had arranged it so. We had expected that he would go to bed in the ordinary way. But he chose this night in which to sit up, and according to the doctor he was about to drop off to sleep in the study.

Grainger went down a third time; but he was hardly out of sight before he was back again with the information that the study was empty and that there was no sign of Martin.

Telling Grainger to stop where he was, I set off as fast as I could towards Sydney's room. I ought to have studied the design of the house much more thoroughly than I had done. I had relied upon Martin's coming to bed, so that he, in whom I felt sure the secret lay, should be under our observation. I had not reckoned on our losing sight of him in this manner.

Reaching the corridor that ended at the door of Sydney's room, I noticed for the first time a dark flight of stone stairs that led downwards, and I realized with horror that this tower, in which I was and in which Sydney was, communicated with the lower floors independently of the main staircase and that anyone could reach Sydney's room without the knowledge of us who had been keeping the main staircase under survey.

I was about to run the last thirty feet or so to Sydney's door, my mind in anguish at the thought that I had not taken the precaution of telling Sydney to remain awake in case of accidents, when I heard the hollow sound of footsteps coming from the old stone stairway.

The corridor was dimly lit from the glow of the night sky, but the stairway was in total darkness. I glanced down it once, then drew back; and as I did so the person ascending reached the top and stepped out slowly into the corridor.

It was Martin. I say so now, but for a moment I did not recognize him, and, all my theories notwithstanding, I shrank back in horror.

He was in a dressing-gown; his hair was ruffled and hanging partly over his eyes, and on his face was such a look of malevolence as I had never before seen on a human visage. His gaze was concentrated in front of him. His underjaw was working, making his teeth grate together audibly. His fingers also were working. He was asleep.

Slowly, but without hesitation, he made for the door of Sydney's room. I followed at a distance on tiptoe.

In the course of my duties I have seen some gruesome and some soul-searing sights, but never have I seen anything that affected me as this did. The effect was akin to that of seeing a brilliant intellect suddenly brought down to mumbling insanity, but this was infinitely more intense for it was crowned by an unspeakable horror.

Martin was not mad. He was acting under the impulse of a very strong volition coming from the unconscious mind—that part of us, imperfectly explored, which retains all the forces of our instincts, He was doing in his sleep that which, when awake, he would hold in abomination. He was no more guilty than we are when we dream. His dreams were deeper than ours, but that is all.

Though I followed him on tiptoe there was no need for me to do so. A noise would be unlikely to wake him, Certainly Sylvia had wakened him the night before when he attacked her; but we must assume that the impulse which drove him to attack Sylvia was not so definite in its intention as that which had driven him to kill Christopher Knight and his own cousin, and which was now

driving him to kill Sydney. He could hardly have had an unconscious desire to kill Sylvia. But these men had the power to deprive him of Sylvia, and nothing short of utter destruction would
satisfy his instincts.

A scientific explanation, however, did nothing to soften the
horror of the moment. The man, as he walked with a measured
step along that corridor in front of me, was an incalculable power
for evil.

At the door he paused and, turning quickly, looked at me.
Rather, he looked through me. And his eyes lit up with the most
unholy ecstasy. Then, with a flourish of exultation, he clutched the
handle of the door and disappeared inside.

I ran forward to follow him into the room; but what was my
horror to find that he had locked the door on the inside!

I shouted. I banged with my fists and kicked with my feet on
the door. I screamed out the name of my son, and continued my
banging and my kicking without waiting for an answer.

Sydney, I knew, was even normally no match for Martin. And
for Sydney to be caught asleep by Martin who, in his present state,
had the strength of ten men was equal to certain death.

But I could hear that a fight of some sort was being put up. A
scuffle was going on within the room. It was something to know
that my son had not been caught by strangling fingers before he
had time to defend himself.

Then I thought of the room next to this one, and hurried into it
in the hope of finding a communicating door between the two. But
there was nothing but the solid wall. I had turned to go to the room
on the other side of Sydney's, in a state that it is unnecessary for
me to try to describe, when I heard a shriek which seemed to reach
me from beyond the window. The shriek was followed by a thud
that made me heave inwardly—the thud of a body on the ground
far below.

It was the body of Martin. I was rushing to the window to look
out, certain that I had been indirectly the cause of my son's death,
when the door of the fatal room was opened with a clatter and
Sydney staggered into the dim light of the corridor.

He could not immediately explain what had happened. The
poor boy was too greatly horrified by what he had experienced.
But by the time the first of the household had come on the scene
he was able to tell me how he had been awakened by someone
who was dragging him out of bed—someone with superhuman
strength. He had struggled—terror, he said, giving him a strength

equal to that of his assailant—and when the struggle was carried across towards the open window it was a question of luck who would go over.

My son is alive to-day, I might remark, only because of Martin's strong instinct of self-preservation. He might have strangled Sydney with the greatest ease in the world, but there was in his unconscious mind that which prompted him to avoid the appearance of murder.

"Where's Martin?" Sydney asked. "Martin warned me about a ghost or something."

"But Martin is dead," I said. "That *was* Martin."

"Martin? That face *Martin's?*"

Sydney's look of incredulity, changing to one of awful horror, made me realize more acutely than anything else the danger in which all who knew the dead man had stood while he was alive.

Two years have passed since these happenings occurred. Sylvia is now my daughter-in-law, and it does seem to be true that time is capable of obliterating the sharpness of even the most intensely painful experiences. And not the least painful of the experiences of that time was the frenzied grief of that queer old man, Makepeace. Fortunately he did not live long to mourn over the end of the House of Strange.

FINIS

RAMBLE HOUSE's

HARRY STEPHEN KEELER WEBWORK MYSTERIES

(RH) indicates the title is available ONLY in the **RAMBLE HOUSE** edition

The Ace of Spades Murder
The Affair of the Bottled Deuce (RH)
The Amazing Web
The Barking Clock
Behind That Mask
The Book with the Orange Leaves
The Bottle with the Green Wax Seal
The Box from Japan
The Case of the Canny Killer
The Case of the Crazy Corpse (RH)
The Case of the Flying Hands (RH)
The Case of the Ivory Arrow
The Case of the Jeweled Ragpicker
The Case of the Lavender Gripsack
The Case of the Mysterious Moll
The Case of the 16 Beans
The Case of the Transparent Nude (RH)
The Case of the Transposed Legs
The Case of the Two-Headed Idiot (RH)
The Case of the Two Strange Ladies
The Circus Stealers (RH)
Cleopatra's Tears
A Copy of Beowulf (RH)
The Crimson Cube (RH)
The Face of the Man From Saturn
Find the Clock
The Five Silver Buddhas
The 4th King
The Gallows Waits, My Lord! (RH)
The Green Jade Hand
Finger! Finger!
Hangman's Nights (RH)
I, Chameleon (RH)
I Killed Lincoln at 10:13! (RH)
The Iron Ring
The Man Who Changed His Skin (RH)
The Man with the Crimson Box
The Man with the Magic Eardrums
The Man with the Wooden Spectacles
The Marceau Case
The Matilda Hunter Murder
The Monocled Monster

The Murder of London Lew
The Murdered Mathematician
The Mysterious Card (RH)
The Mysterious Ivory Ball of Wong Shing Li (RH)
The Mystery of the Fiddling Cracksman
The Peacock Fan
The Photo of Lady X (RH)
The Portrait of Jirjohn Cobb
Report on Vanessa Hewstone (RH)
Riddle of the Travelling Skull
Riddle of the Wooden Parrakeet (RH)
The Scarlet Mummy (RH)
The Search for X-Y-Z
The Sharkskin Book
Sing Sing Nights
The Six From Nowhere (RH)
The Skull of the Waltzing Clown
The Spectacles of Mr. Cagliostro
Stand By—London Calling!
The Steeltown Strangler
The Stolen Gravestone (RH)
Strange Journey (RH)
The Strange Will
The Straw Hat Murders (RH)
The Street of 1000 Eyes (RH)
Thieves' Nights
Three Novellos (RH)
The Tiger Snake
The Trap (RH)
Vagabond Nights (Defrauded Yeggman)
Vagabond Nights 2 (10 Hours)
The Vanishing Gold Truck
The Voice of the Seven Sparrows
The Washington Square Enigma
When Thief Meets Thief
The White Circle (RH)
The Wonderful Scheme of Mr. Christopher Thorne
X. Jones—of Scotland Yard
Y. Cheung, Business Detective

Keeler Related Works

A To Izzard: A Harry Stephen Keeler Companion by Fender Tucker — Articles and stories about Harry, by Harry, and in his style. Included is a compleat bibliography.

Wild About Harry: Reviews of Keeler Novels — Edited by Richard Polt & Fender Tucker — 22 reviews of works by Harry Stephen Keeler from *Keeler News*. A perfect introduction to the author.

The Keeler Keyhole Collection: Annotated newsletter rants from Harry Stephen Keeler, edited by Francis M. Nevins. Over 400 pages of incredibly personal Keeleriana.

Fakealoo — Pastiches of the style of Harry Stephen Keeler by selected demented members of the HSK Society. Updated every year with the new winner.

RAMBLE HOUSE's OTHER LOONS

The End of It All and Other Stories — Ed Gorman's latest short story collection

Four Dancing Tuatara Press Books — *Beast or Man?* By Sean M'Guire; *The Whistling Ancestors* by Richard E. Goddard; *The Shadow on the House* and *Sorcerer's Chessmen* by Mark Hansom. With introductions by John Pelan.

The Dumpling — Political murder from 1907 by Coulson Kernahan

Victims & Villains — Intriguing Sherlockiana from Derham Groves

Evidence in Blue — 1938 mystery by E. Charles Vivian

The Case of the Little Green Men — Mack Reynolds wrote this love song to sci-fi fans back in 1951 and it's now back in print.

Hell Fire — A new hard-boiled novel by Jack Moskovitz about an arsonist, an arson cop and a Nazi hooker. It isn't pretty.

Researching American-Made Toy Soldiers — A 276-page collection of a lifetime of articles by toy soldier expert Richard O'Brien

Strands of the Web: Short Stories of Harry Stephen Keeler — Edited and Introduced by Fred Cleaver

The Sam McCain Novels — Ed Gorman's terrific series includes *The Day the Music Died, Wake Up Little Susie* and *Will You Still Love Me Tomorrow?*

A Shot Rang Out — Three decades of reviews from Jon Breen

Mysterious Martin, the Master of Murder — Two versions of a strange 1912 novel by Tod Robbins about a man who writes books that can kill.

Dago Red — 22 tales of dark suspense by Bill Pronzini

The Night Remembers — A 1991 Jack Walsh mystery from Ed Gorman

Rough Cut & New, Improved Murder — Ed Gorman's first two novels

Hollywood Dreams — A novel of the Depression by Richard O'Brien

Seven Gelett Burgess Novels — *The Master of Mysteries, The White Cat, Two O'Clock Courage, Ladies in Boxes, Find the Woman, The Heart Line, The Picaroons*

The Organ Reader — A huge compilation of just about everything published in the 1971-1972 radical bay-area newspaper, *THE ORGAN*.

A Clear Path to Cross — Sharon Knowles short mystery stories by Ed Lynskey

Old Times' Sake — Short stories by James Reasoner from Mike Shayne Magazine

Freaks and Fantasies — Eerie tales by Tod Robbins, collaborator of Tod Browning on the film FREAKS.

Six Jim Harmon Double Novels — *Vixen Hollow/Celluloid Scandal, The Man Who Made Maniacs/Silent Siren, Ape Rape/Wanton Witch, Sex Burns Like Fire/Twist Session, Sudden Lust/Passion Strip, Sin Unlimited/Harlot Master, Twilight Girls/Sex Institution.* Written in the early 60s.

Marblehead: A Novel of H.P. Lovecraft — A long-lost masterpiece from Richard A. Lupoff. Published for the first time!

The Compleat Ova Hamlet — Parodies of SF authors by Richard A. Lupoff – A brand new edition with more stories and more illustrations by Trina Robbins

The Secret Adventures of Sherlock Holmes — Three Sherlockian pastiches by the Brooklyn author/publisher, Gary Lovisi.

The Universal Holmes — Richard A. Lupoff's 2007 collection of five Holmesian pastiches and a recipe for giant rat stew.

Four Joel Townsley Rogers Novels — By the author of *The Red Right Hand: Once In a Red Moon, Lady With the Dice, The Stopped Clock, Never Leave My Bed*

Two Joel Townsley Rogers Story Collections — Night of Horror and Killing Time

Twenty Norman Berrow Novels — *The Bishop's Sword, Ghost House, Don't Go Out After Dark, Claws of the Cougar, The Smokers of Hashish, The Secret Dancer, Don't Jump Mr. Boland!, The Footprints of Satan, Fingers for Ransom, The Three Tiers of Fantasy, The Spaniard's Thumb, The Eleventh Plague, Words Have Wings, One Thrilling Night, The Lady's in Danger, It Howls at Night, The Terror in the Fog, Oil Under the Window, Murder in the Melody, The Singing Room*

The N. R. De Mexico Novels — Robert Bragg presents *Marijuana Girl, Madman on a Drum, Private Chauffeur* in one volume.

Four Chelsea Quinn Yarbro Novels featuring Charlie Moon — *Ogilvie, Tallant and Moon, Music When the Sweet Voice Dies, Poisonous Fruit* and *Dead Mice*

Five Walter S. Masterman Mysteries — *The Green Toad, The Flying Beast, The Yellow Mistletoe, The Wrong Verdict* and *The Perjured Alibi.* Fantastic impossible plots.

Two Hake Talbot Novels — *Rim of the Pit, The Hangman's Handyman.* Classic locked room mysteries.

Two Alexander Laing Novels — *The Motives of Nicholas Holtz* and *Dr. Scarlett,* stories of medical mayhem and intrigue from the 30s.

Four David Hume Novels — *Corpses Never Argue, Cemetery First Stop, Make Way for the Mourners, Eternity Here I Come*, and more to come.

Three Wade Wright Novels — *Echo of Fear, Death At Nostalgia Street* and *It Leads to Murder*, with more to come!

Eight Rupert Penny Novels — *Policeman's Holiday, Policeman's Evidence, Lucky Policeman, Policeman in Armour, Sealed Room Murder, Sweet Poison, The Talkative Policeman, She had to Have Gas* and *Cut and Run* (by Martin Tanner.)

Five Jack Mann Novels — Strange murder in the English countryside. *Gees' First Case, Nightmare Farm, Grey Shapes, The Ninth Life, The Glass Too Many.*

Seven Max Afford Novels — *Owl of Darkness, Death's Mannikins, Blood on His Hands, The Dead Are Blind, The Sheep and the Wolves, Sinners in Paradise* and *Two Locked Room Mysteries and a Ripping Yarn* by one of Australia's finest novelists.

Five Joseph Shallit Novels — *The Case of the Billion Dollar Body, Lady Don't Die on My Doorstep, Kiss the Killer, Yell Bloody Murder, Take Your Last Look.* One of America's best 50's authors.

Two Crimson Clown Novels — By Johnston McCulley, author of the Zorro novels, *The Crimson Clown* and *The Crimson Clown Again.*

The Best of 10-Story Book — edited by Chris Mikul, over 35 stories from the literary magazine Harry Stephen Keeler edited.

A Young Man's Heart — A forgotten early classic by Cornell Woolrich

The Anthony Boucher Chronicles — edited by Francis M. Nevins
Book reviews by Anthony Boucher written for the *San Francisco Chronicle,* 1942 – 1947. Essential and fascinating reading.

Muddled Mind: Complete Works of Ed Wood, Jr. — David Hayes and Hayden Davis deconstruct the life and works of a mad genius.

Gadsby — A lipogram (a novel without the letter E). Ernest Vincent Wright's last work, published in 1939 right before his death.

My First Time: The One Experience You Never Forget — Michael Birchwood — 64 true first-person narratives of how they lost it.

A Roland Daniel Double: The Signal and The Return of Wu Fang — Classic thrillers from the 30s

Murder in Shawnee — Two novels of the Alleghenies by John Douglas: *Shawnee Alley Fire* and *Haunts.*

Deep Space and other Stories — A collection of SF gems by Richard A. Lupoff

Blood Moon — The first of the Robert Payne series by Ed Gorman

The Time Armada — Fox B. Holden's 1953 SF gem.

Black River Falls — Suspense from the master, Ed Gorman

Sideslip — 1968 SF masterpiece by Ted White and Dave Van Arnam

The Triune Man — Mindscrambling science fiction from Richard A. Lupoff

Detective Duff Unravels It — Episodic mysteries by Harvey O'Higgins

Automaton — Brilliant treatise on robotics: 1928-style! By H. Stafford Hatfield

The Incredible Adventures of Rowland Hern — Rousing 1928 impossible crimes by Nicholas Olde.

Slammer Days — Two full-length prison memoirs: *Men into Beasts* (1952) by George Sylvester Viereck and *Home Away From Home* (1962) by Jack Woodford

Murder in Black and White — 1931 classic tennis whodunit by Evelyn Elder

Killer's Caress — Cary Moran's 1936 hardboiled thriller

The Golden Dagger — 1951 Scotland Yard yarn by E. R. Punshon

A Smell of Smoke — 1951 English countryside thriller by Miles Burton

Ruled By Radio — 1925 futuristic novel by Robert L. Hadfield & Frank E. Farncombe

Murder in Silk — A 1937 Yellow Peril novel of the silk trade by Ralph Trevor

The Case of the Withered Hand — 1936 potboiler by John G. Brandon

Finger-prints Never Lie — A 1939 classic detective novel by John G. Brandon

Inclination to Murder — 1966 thriller by New Zealand's Harriet Hunter

Invaders from the Dark — Classic werewolf tale from Greye La Spina

Fatal Accident — Murder by automobile, a 1936 mystery by Cecil M. Wills

The Devil Drives — A prison and lost treasure novel by Virgil Markham

Dr. Odin — Douglas Newton's 1933 potboiler comes back to life.

The Chinese Jar Mystery — Murder in the manor by John Stephen Strange, 1934

The Julius Caesar Murder Case — A classic 1935 re-telling of the assassination by Wallace Irwin that's much more fun than the Shakespeare version

West Texas War and Other Western Stories — by Gary Lovisi

The Contested Earth and Other SF Stories — A never-before published space opera and seven short stories by Jim Harmon.

Tales of the Macabre and Ordinary — Modern twisted horror by Chris Mikul, author of the *Bizarrism* series.

The Gold Star Line — Seaboard adventure from L.T. Reade and Robert Eustace.

The Werewolf vs the Vampire Woman — Hard to believe ultraviolence by either Arthur M. Scarm or Arthur M. Scram.

Black Hogan Strikes Again — Australia's Peter Renwick pens a tale of the outback.

Don Diablo: Book of a Lost Film — Two-volume treatment of a western by Paul Landres, with diagrams. Intro by Francis M. Nevins.

The Charlie Chaplin Murder Mystery — Movie hijinks by Wes D. Gehring

The Koky Comics — A collection of all of the 1978-1981 Sunday and daily comic strips by Richard O'Brien and Mort Gerberg, in two volumes.

Suzy — Another collection of comic strips from Richard O'Brien and Bob Vojtko.

Dime Novels: Ramble House's 10-Cent Books — *Knife in the Dark* by Robert Leslie Bellem, *Hot Lead* and *Song of Death* by Ed Earl Repp, *A Hashish House in New York* by H.H. Kane, and five more.

Blood in a Snap — The *Finnegan's Wake* of the 21st century, by Jim Weiler

Stakeout on Millennium Drive — Award-winning Indianapolis Noir — Ian Woollen.

Dope Tales #1 — Two dope-riddled classics; *Dope Runners* by Gerald Grantham and *Death Takes the Joystick* by Phillip Condé.

Dope Tales #2 — Two more narco-classics; *The Invisible Hand* by Rex Dark and *The Smokers of Hashish* by Norman Berrow.

Dope Tales #3 — Two enchanting novels of opium by the master, Sax Rohmer. *Dope* and *The Yellow Claw*.

Tenebrae — Ernest G. Henham's 1898 horror tale brought back.

The Singular Problem of the Stygian House-Boat — Two classic tales by John Kendrick Bangs about the denizens of Hades.

Tiresias — Psychotic modern horror novel by Jonathan M. Sweet.

The One After Snelling — Kickass modern noir from Richard O'Brien.

The Sign of the Scorpion — 1935 Edmund Snell tale of oriental evil.

The House of the Vampire — 1907 poetic thriller by George S. Viereck.

An Angel in the Street — Modern hardboiled noir by Peter Genovese.

The Devil's Mistress — Scottish gothic tale by J. W. Brodie-Innes.

The Lord of Terror — 1925 mystery with master-criminal, Fantômas.

The Lady of the Terraces — 1925 adventure by E. Charles Vivian.

My Deadly Angel — 1955 Cold War drama by John Chelton.

Prose Bowl — Futuristic satire — Bill Pronzini & Barry N. Malzberg .

Satan's Den Exposed — True crime in Truth or Consequences New Mexico — Award-winning journalism by the *Desert Journal*.

The Amorous Intrigues & Adventures of Aaron Burr — by Anonymous — Hot historical action.

I Stole $16,000,000 — A true story by cracksman Herbert E. Wilson.

The Black Dark Murders — Vintage 50s college murder yarn by Milt Ozaki, writing as Robert O. Saber.

Sex Slave — Potboiler of lust in the days of Cleopatra — Dion Leclerq.

You'll Die Laughing — Bruce Elliott's 1945 novel of murder at a practical joker's English countryside manor.

The Private Journal & Diary of John H. Surratt — The memoirs of the man who conspired to assassinate President Lincoln.

Dead Man Talks Too Much — Hollywood boozer by Weed Dickenson

Red Light — History of legal prostitution in Shreveport Louisiana by Eric Brock. Includes wonderful photos of the houses and the ladies.

A Snark Selection — Lewis Carroll's *The Hunting of the Snark* with two Snarkian chapters by Harry Stephen Keeler — Illustrated by Gavin L. O'Keefe.

Ripped from the Headlines! — The Jack the Ripper story as told in the newspaper articles in the *New York* and *London Times*.

Geronimo — S. M. Barrett's 1905 autobiography of a noble American.

The White Peril in the Far East — Sidney Lewis Gulick's 1905 indictment of the West and assurance that Japan would never attack the U.S.

The Compleat Calhoon — All of Fender Tucker's works: Includes *Totah Six-Pack, Weed, Women and Song* and *Tales from the Tower,* plus a CD of all of his songs.

Totah Six-Pack — Just Fender Tucker's six tales about Farmington in one sleek volume.

RAMBLE HOUSE

Fender Tucker, Prop.

www.ramblehouse.com   fender@ramblehouse.com

228-826-1783   10329 Sheephead Drive, Vancleave MS 39565

www.ingramcontent.com/pod-product-compliance
Lightning Source LLC
Chambersburg PA
CBHW030333020726
47493CB00004B/1257